SPANGLE

Second Edition

For my brother and sister

Suzanne J Davies

3

SPANGLE

2016

Fitting that it should be raining. Fine, drizzly, intangible rain that the automatic windscreen wipers on my little Japanese car don't quite know how to deal with. But I'm not driving so it's a minor inconvenience, being parked just a few yards along from the house trying to see and not be seen.

I feel as if I am prying but there's no reason to feel exposed. He has no idea what car I may have or whether or not I can drive for that matter. Besides, I could be anyone. Observing in my glass and metal sanctuary. Obscured behind rain- dashed, misted windows. No faces at the windows. The houses in the street blank. Unseeing.

Are the old neighbours still living here I wonder? Doreen, Shirley, would any of them recognise me?

I turn the engine off and look properly at the house. The rectangular box the same but so different. The brutal pebble dash on the side wall painted over with a thick creamy yellow gloop. The grit covered and softened. The stylish metal porch frame gone, rebuilt as a much larger brick and plastic construction with a tiled roof, a side window and little cloakroom inside. A rubber plant basking happily on the sill.

The changes to the house are standard but I feel shocked, even slightly violated by the fact of most of the side garden having been dug away and flattened out as a parking space for their flashy, expensive but free motability car. This years' registration. The staggered redbrick wall we climbed on and jumped off protecting it on the far side.

4

Apart from that wall nothing else remains of the garden I loved and played in, not a patch of lawn left. The grass I cartwheeled across, the tree my brother fell from, gone, covered over with pink, grey and lemon crazy paving topped with shrubs in mis-matched coloured plastic pots. Mum's flower beds vanished. The gate we got told off for swinging on, disappeared.

Jutting out at the side, a tasteless plastic conservatory sprawls across the back wall of the house behind the kitchen. Bedecked with fringed blinds, a glimpse of bamboo furniture inside. I think I can see a newspaper on the arm of the nearest chair. Spectacles on top.

They are elderly now. Respect your elders, he would have said. Silver haired, he puts up with the unpleasantness of gout and she with the nagging pain of rheumatoid arthritis. Illness and temperament meant neither could hold down jobs. Still the evidence suggests they have managed very comfortably on their disability benefits, pensions and inheritances. Other people's money. Much of it spent transforming the house. Our house.

I suddenly register that they will die there. Florid and overweight. Rooted in until the bitter end.

I feel an involuntary shiver and turn the engine back on to restart the heater. This was only our home for a few short years, theirs for decades, but it feels wrong, an injustice even. They have replaced furniture, changed fittings and decorated it many times. Knocked down walls and re-arranged the rooms. They have given it their stamp, erased us from it.

Or do they sometimes feel our ghosts in there with them? Do we haunt them? Like this house haunts me. Pulls me back to it. A random work trip means that today I unexpectedly passed near-by. Too near-by to not take the turn off the Ring Road that never used to exist. Too near-by to not drive slowly past the rain glistening beech hedge enclosing the Chapel and then to turn down into Oak Hill and onto the street, our street, past the green to take a look.

PART ONE

1976

Forever and Ever

"Forever and ever and ever and ever

You'll be the one

Who shines on me like the morning sun."

CHAPTER ONE

My Mummy, Julie was like the sunshine. She had a trusting, open smile that bought warmth on the coldest day, she loved and she laughed easily. She had a luminescence and she shone on everyone, like the morning sun in the haunting song that wafted exotically to number one in the hit parade in the heat exploding summer of 1976.

Although that was never one of my favourites, transient pop songs were the weft and warp of my growing up years and they helped us kids map the adult worlds of love and pain.

So if my Mummy was the morning sun, then my Daddy cast a shadow over all of us. He was the black cloud that raced suddenly across the sky and cast all in shade on a bright sunny day, then skittered off as fast as it had arrived. He was sarcastic and caustic. Hurtful and hateful and then cracked a joke and was gone. Even when we were doing nice things together like looking at photographs of their wedding day he was unable to say anything that wasn't in some way barbed.

"You look so beautiful Mummy. That's a lovely dress." I say looking at one of the larger monochrome full-length pictures of just the two of them. And of course, she did look beautiful in an Audrey Hepburn style taffeta gown with her neat dark auburn beehive held in place with a matching headband. Mummy was smiling serenely at the camera, her huge heavily lashed eyes aglow with happiness.

"Yep, it's amazing what you could pick up in C&A in those days" Daddy interjected. "Do you know what C&A stands for Spangle?" I shook my head having no idea what he was getting at, "Cheap and awful, har har har cheap and bloody awful like your mother."

"Don't be rude Brian, anyway your mother made me that dress, you couldn't put a value on what that dress means to me."

"Well that's the truth, a shop bought dress wouldn't have gone round your belly would it? See Spangle you are in that photo as well, under that very dress. That's why your Mother looks so swell!" He guffawed to himself as we carried on leafing through the pages of the beautifully bound wedding album.

There were a few more set piece photographs and by and large my Mummy's was the only smiling face in most of them, though Daddy's best man was smirking drunkenly in quite a few. Nanna's face was solemn and Mummy's parents looked ashen. Though smartly dressed and groomed they gave the appearance of having been kidnapped from somewhere else and dumped in a grotty registry office against their will.

"It was a very romantic day Brian. The service was, well formal but meaningful. Forever and ever, til death do us part. Why do you always have to be so rude?" Mummy said.

"Yes Julie, dear, a very nice day." he said in his sarcastic tone.

"The happiest day of your life?" Mummy ventured to ask.

"Of course. Never had so many people buying me free pints in one day before or since, so of course it was the happiest day of my life." He laughed, put his paper down, looked at his watch and said, "Speaking of which, opening time." And he disappeared off out.

Although their wedding album screamed vintage sixties, Daddy looking quite the mod with his winkle pickers and trim tonic suit, their marriage was pure nineteen seventies.

Remember that decade, that decade of irony? Affordable electronic home appliances juxtaposed with national power cuts. Ordinary people enjoying vastly improved social and physical mobility with more affordable cars on the roads whilst

British car plants were being callously shut down. Barbed black humour. Sexism, racism and every other ism not named but taken as read. My father was a 70s man through and through. He was very comfortable in that decade. It suited him. Bitter, twisted and brown. His mousey hair with sideburns, his synthetic suits and his dark driving leather gloves, even though we didn't have a car. Brian Reid, apart from his often purply, red sweaty face, was a tribute to the colour scheme of the times. Like one of those card strips you bought home from Woolworths when you were choosing new paint. Every nuanced shade of brown included, going from dark to light to lighter.

Daddy loved his pop music, though he had different tastes to my mother. He would turn the radio up full blast if any of his favourites came on. He loved the Beatles and the Kinks and was proud of his working-class taste in music. In fact he had a genuine interest in all forms of popular culture, from the adverts in the television breaks to the editorials in the Daily Mail. He was quick, sparky and was always cracking jokes about Frank Bough, the TUC and the common market. For a long-haired working-class shop lad he was remarkably well informed about current affairs and he had plenty to say on the articles he read in his daily newspapers. He never missed the tea-time television news, if he was home, and he had plenty of droll comments that he enjoyed throwing out into the ether.

"Cod wars! No one gets between me and me fish fingers eh Spangle? They can tell that to the Fisheries Minister- we know where he keeps his money don't we? In a riverbank! Geddit? In a riverbank." Daddy saw himself as a rakish combination of both the modern men who were the 'Likely Lads' which was his favourite telly programme.

"I should have me own programme on the telly I should." He would say. Even I have to admit, his acerbic sarcasm did hit the spot sometimes. Funnier than Les Dawson anyway.

1970s life was contoured and coloured by a river of silt leaving its tidemark of earthy pigments on everyone's daily accoutrements, three-piece suites, soft furnishings, crockery, shoes, clothes and even most people's hair.

Maybe that's part of what made me and my little brother a bit different from our friends and neighbours and most other people around us. Because although Mummy's hair was a lustrous deep chestnut and Daddy's was a dull pale tan, our hair, mine and Michael's was a shocking Scandinavian white gold. It was long too. I could sit on mine and Michael's skirted his shoulders giving him the look of an angelic page boy who had been dragged through a hedge backwards. He was always flicking a rogue curl out of his eyes. People would stop my mother to comment on our golden hair when we were out and about. Perfect strangers would come up to Mummy in Fine Fare to make a remark, sometimes even asking if they could touch it. Or worse, some people would just touch it without asking. Often people would mistake my brother for a little girl and Mummy would bristle if Daddy was in earshot as this was sure to inflame him.

It was discernible that people saw our family as distinct or even peculiar. Or was that just how it felt? Perhaps every family felt different from the inside.

Different or not, the Reids did fully partake in the same home styling trends as everyone else. Whilst Daddy didn't really notice or care, as long as the house was clean, which it always was, Mummy giddyingly embraced the whole 70s ambience. Our new house in Loxwood new town totally showcased those popular contemporary hues. Mummy did audaciously experiment with what she called 'accent colours' like blinding orange or sage green but we might as well have had dirt in our fingernails and worn dungarees with all the mud tones everywhere.

There is a lot to be said for mud. Soil is fertility, a source of life. But it is also the stuff we bury ourselves under when we die. The soil without the suns' warmth loses its ability to produce and nurture life. Having said that, my little brother Michael used to eat mud so I don't know what, if any, significance there is in that!

Michael would often sit alone on the garden path, golden head down, in his worn cords and brown and orange hand knitted jumper digging away with an old kitchen spoon at the soil under the grass at its edge. He would poke out worms and examine them with his dirty fingers. I don't know if he really ate the mud or just rubbed his mouth with his mucky hands and that it looked like that. When I took his arm to bring him in to wash and I asked him if he had been eating mud he didn't reply. He was in a world of his own, that boy, that's all I do know. A world of his own.

Mine and Michaels daily life was also lived in the palette of brown but even the homes of the better off were flamboyantly drab then and no amount of dipped earthenware, macramé or string pin art could change that. The financially comfortable families did enjoy some interesting, quirky material goods such as electric carving knives and heated hair rollers, alien looking contraptions we only saw on the prize filled conveyor belt on 'The Generation Game'. Not even a fridge or colour TV for us when we first moved to Little Loxwood. Though we had a boxy black and white, which, to my father, was far more important than a getting a fridge because he still preferred his beer warm and his snooker monochrome.

The Reid family were running to keep up with the aspirations of the time with most of Daddy's wages being directed towards supporting the British Brewing industry. But at least we had finally left behind the outside toilet of the crumbling terrace. Instead of cobwebs and a draughty gap under the door we now had, in addition to our bathroom, a separate toilet at the top of the stairs. The bonneted dolly on the window sill, whose pink and yellow crocheted dress hid the spare toilet roll, was a surreal housewarming present from Nanna who must have made it to mock her son's debauched inadequacies as he stood at eye level to its perfect plastic face whilst splashing away his toxic waste from the night before.

Our new house in Little Loxwood offered many luxuries. For Mummy it was a definite step up, a chance of a better life. God knows she deserved it. Before moving here we had been living in a shabby, decayed two up two down but before that, when my brother was only really a tiny baby, we had lived with my Daddy's Mummy, Nanna.

Nanna's post war, pre-fabricated, shell pink bungalow had small rooms with high ceilings and the inside walls were papery as if made from thick cardboard, but somehow we had all fitted in. Nanna had such a fondness for the place having lived there for well over twenty years already. These temporary homes soon becoming a lot more permanent than originally intended. Nanna and Grampy had been offered their home when he came back from the war, injured and homeless and though he had died not many years after, she had lived there ever since.

"They'll take me out of here in my coffin." I had heard Nanna say to a range of callers from a young gypsy boy selling chamoise leathers, to the tired and shabby looking man from the Pru. Anyone who would listen. The dinky pastel construction was joined to another, its mirror image which had been painted pale grey and there was another pair the same next door to that, one lemon and the other white. They had come in kits and been squeezed in on some wasteland at the end of a short street of 1930s houses. The prefabs' dwellers had customised them over the years by painting them in their preferred but always pastel shades. They each had net-curtained windows and sat in the middle of verdant, colourful, well-tended gardens. There was something neat, harmonious and unusual about the little foursome. Days in the terrace in town were chilly but in the tiny bungalow they had been congenial and warm.

"I can't see how this pattern is going to work out Mum. It doesn't look like the picture." Aunty Cathy turned the magazine photograph sideways to get a better look.

"This bit is only the border, you need to imagine it going all the way around. It's tricky because it's a semi-circle" my Mummy tried to patiently explain to her sister in-law.

"We just need to keep alternating the amber and the gold for three more rows and then it will start to make sense. We used this very same pattern at the Townswomen's Guild last year and it came out beautifully." Nanna said.

"Hmm" said Aunty Cathy taking a puff of her fag. "If you say so Mother!"

"Can you check on Michael for me Spangle?" Mummy asked.

I did as I was told as they continued to loop pieces of yarn around a hook and thread it through a huge unwieldy piece of canvas sacking. Each of them had a hunk of the fabric on their laps and they were working inwards towards the centre.

Michael was fast asleep on the settle in the kitchen so I was especially quiet so as not to wake him. Marmalade, Nanna's cat was at his feet. The long galley kitchen was so much warmer than the living room as even on a grey day like today the light poured in through the large windows which ran the length of the back of the bungalow. I don't know how Mummy, Nanna and Aunty Cathy could even see what they were doing back there in that dark sitting room at the front of the house. They were making a woollen rug from a kit but the holes in the fabric were quite small and the colours very similar to each other so the complex pattern of graph squares and crosses was not easy to follow. Despite this Nanna would not let anyone switch a light or any other electrical appliance on in the prefab until after six pm due to her morbid fear of high electricity bills and having her supply cut off. Luckily the kettle set to boil on the gas hob so a constant supply of tea kept everyone going.

14

Daddy would be home from work soon and Mummy would cook a family meal. The atmosphere would change and the bungalow would feel more constrained and claustrophobic.

"It's for your bottom drawer Cathy so I hope you'll like it." Nanna was saying when I came back in.

"In that case, there's no hurry." laughed Aunty Cathy throwing her head back and tossing her pretty red curls so they glinted in a shimmer of early evening light.

"I think you should give it to Julie and Brian if they get their new house." she said magnanimously.

"If!" my Mummy said a little wistfully. "The man at the corporation says the waiting list has hardly gone down since we were added. I feel like giving up sometimes. I've said to Brian we should rent in town until a corporation tenancy comes up but he says we can't afford it."

"Just have patience Julie and keep praying to the good Lord." Nanna said.

"I'm sure it won't be much longer Julie. I'd love to live round there. Nice and clean and open. Just right for you and the kids. Anyway, keep your fingers crossed. Well, I need to straighten myself out and get back to my digs Mum, before it gets too dark. I'll pop in on you tomorrow." I could see the affection in her face as Aunty Cathy gave my Nanna a peck on the top of her grey netted head. She seemed so grown up to me though she was only a teenager then.

"See you Julie, see you Spangle!" Aunty Cathy said as she buttoned up her quilted anorak and fastened her headscarf in a tight knot at her neck against the drizzle outside.

Mummy got up and saw her to the door then went back to the kitchen to see to the baby. She carried Michael into his cot in the second bedroom of the bungalow that she and Michael shared with my Daddy. It was a panelled square shaped bedroom that used to be Aunty Cathy's. Nanna had no truck with the trend for brown. The room was painted a violet colour and had blue and lavender curtains. There was speckled grey lino on the floor. I stood at the door jamb and watched Mummy tuck her baby in to his little metal cot. An ancient saggy double bed within a huge dark wooden frame took up most of the floor space with my brothers' cot tucked tightly under the window.

"Into the bathroom with you, young lady." she said to me when he was snug.

"I've been thinking Gwen." I heard Mummy say as I diligently scrubbed away at my baby teeth in the dark bathroom. "I'm going to talk to Brian again about us finding a place of our own. Even if it's a bit further out. Anything will do. Us all being here is not fair on you, or Cathy. Those digs she has to put up with, sharing a bathroom with all sorts. She could be back here in her own home if we moved out."

I savoured the gentle mintyness of the toothpaste as I carefully made sure not to miss a single millimetre of my teeths' enamel. The streetlight outside twinkled through the dimpled glass of the bathroom window. I didn't catch Nanna's reply or the conversations Mummy must have had with Daddy about it later but it wasn't much longer afterwards that we did leave the bungalow though Aunty Cathy never did move back in.

CHAPTER TWO

The house Mummy found in town was bleak and permanently chilly, even though she did let us use the electric bar fire when Daddy was out. Mummy said it was characterful, a back to back, a two up two down. Daddy said it was a slum not fit for cockroaches and it was not his bloody idea to live here.

Michael was too little to say anything and I silently rued the biting cold, not daring to vocalise it, knowing it would cause an argument. We did have a paraffin heater upstairs on the landing, the smell of it reassuring and heady. But it could not permeate the iciness and we endured the discomfort of wearing hats, socks and jumpers to bed.

Without Nanna and without Aunty Cathy popping in the atmosphere was cold too. Mummy and Daddy argued more in this house. Doors got slammed. Chairs got thrown around and occasional bits of crockery were hurled and smashed after Daddy came in late from the pub. One morning Mummy was sat crying in the kitchen after he had gone off to work. She had a bruise around her eye but she flashed us one of her sunshine smiles as we came in to that cold flag-stoned kitchen. She flicked the radio on and set about making us breakfast.

The letter box rattled as she picked Michael up and placed him into his highchair ready to be spoon-fed Weetabix and warm milk. I ran to get the post, a solitary brown envelope, crisp and with a cellophane window displaying our family name and address.

Mummy's hands trembled as she opened it. It was the letter she had been waiting for.

My mother's dream house sat on what was once cultivated farmland in a wide river valley dotted with and surrounded by woodland. Now a brick and concrete housing estate, artefacts and traces of human settlements had been found here predating Roman times. When we excitedly moved in it had been up for less than a decade. The area had been populated since ancient times but it had a newness. It was for the working classes but definitely not somewhere that could be described as a slum like the area our two up two down was in.

"Look Bri, it's sooo modern! O the size of this sitting room. That's what is known as a double aspect. Window at the front and at the back of the same room. Bit of woodchip on the long wall would be just right. Ripple texture, you know." Daddy said nothing. My Mummy cooed at and through the serving hatch, the airing cupboard and what she called a coat room in the under stairs cupboard in the hallway. The piece de resistance caused Mummy to exclaim, ecstatically on discovering the tiny toilet separate and next door to the little but more than adequate bathroom, "O Lord, privacy at last!"

"Brian do you think the twintub will fit in under this counter, erm I mean under the breakfast bar?" Daddy threw her a quizzical look as Mummy pointed to a formica topped shelf crossing the far side wall of the kitchen, tucked between the pantry wall and the backdoor.

"I am sure I can get it in and still have room for a couple of high stools." She continued. Daddy nodded, approving of this new phrase, breakfast bar, that Mummy had just come up with. She continued to talk to herself as she worked out where our meagre possessions could go and how she would make use of all this extra living-space. Daddy grunted at most of these exclamations. He had already reckied the pub and felt that it would adequately meet his standards. He dutifully poked his head into the built-in wardrobes and clambered up to look vacantly into the loft and whilst his face clearly said that he would rather have been anywhere but here, with us, and if my mother wanted woodchip she would be putting it up herself, he still went straight over to the council offices in town centre that same afternoon and signed on the dotted line.

18

Within a semi-circular grid of other new homes, sat the new Reid residence, number 11 Sycamore Drive. Red and grey brick to the front and back and grey, black and silver pebble dash on the side and although the houses were by no means all identical to one another they had a uniformity of style. A rigidity that suggested they could have been built out of Lego. Original, basic Lego, with a solid, rectangular base, uniform rectangular windows and doors and well, solid rectangular bricks.

What a contrast to the deprived dirty streets that we were moving away from. The stone terraced workers homes had plenty of character but comfort over charm was what a young family needed. Mod cons.

It had been in that run-down town that Mummy and Daddy had first caught each other's eye. In a house very like the one we had lived in for that cold short time. Without ever having met before, without ever having previously said a word to her Brian had bought across one of my Mummy's first ever alcoholic drinks at a college party he had gate-crashed. He had found out the name of the 'dolly bird' in the green dress from another party goer, then navigated a glass of Babycham and his own bottle of beer across the small crowded room, confidently smelling of the Old Spice his mother had bought him for Christmas. He gave the beautiful dark-haired girl the drink. She smiled shyly, he smiled boldly. He tilted his head, gave her a wink and said, "You've just met your Romeo, Julliette." And she fell for it, forgetting just how badly that particular love story had turned out. Knowing nothing at all about him except what he looked and smelt like.

Good-looking youngsters, adrift and finding their way. Mummy had been a hairdressing student until she fell pregnant with me not so long after that fateful night. Before she ever had a chance to get to know him, Brian, the Romeo. Before she realised that Daddy wasn't a student and never went to the college. Before she knew that he was a chancer trying to find the job that paid the most for doing the least and for which no skills or qualifications were required. Before she knew what the back of his hand felt like but how his words could hurt even more than the sting of his signet ring on her pretty ivory cheek.

But this house move, a secure tenancy, in a nice area, Mummy knew this could give them a touch of respectability. It could remove the taint of growing up in a pre-fab, fatherless, the smear of living in a slum. My mother was sure this was just what my Daddy needed and she was happy and she shone even brighter. "Little Loxwood is a very desirable area. It's the nicest estate in Loxwood." I had heard Mummy gushing to Nanna as they discussed our planned move.

"With Brian's new job and the subsidised rents I really do think we can afford it!" she added. Nanna replied in her dour Presbyterian way that she had always believed that the good Lord would provide but from her face she looked pleased too. Little Loxwood was closer to her bungalow than our old place so it would be easier for her to visit us.

"I hope it all goes through Julie. Be lovely for the children." Nanna was genuinely pleased for us.

"They will have a garden to play in Gwen. It's just perfect."

"There's a handsome new Methodist Chapel there too." Nanna went on. "Mrs Price attends, says it's a smart modern building. It has its own community hall. Lovely services, she's told me all about the Minister, very kind man. It's well-attended and I am sure you will find it welcoming."

Michael and I exchanged doubtful glances.

Just as I mapped out the world according to pop songs, Nanna made sense of everything through Chapel. Chapel provided her reference points for all of life's experiences. "They have a very nice Sunday school, Spangle! Much nicer than the one at Crossridge. The children there are a bit rough!"

This so called 'new town' was really five quite old villages that had been joined together in a planned way throughout the 1950s and 60s. Although the wider town was called Loxwood the original village names remained for the estates of Crossridge, Little Loxwood, Norton, Loxley and Brockham. It would be fair to say that there was a degree of rivalry between their residents.

The pedestrianised town centre that united them had a glossy purpose-built department store and all the popular shops and between us and it was a belt of factories which followed the railway and which meant jobs and prosperity. There was a car parts factory and a biscuit factory where Wagon Wheels and Jammy Dodgers were made. Depending on wind direction you could sometimes smell the biscuits baking from the school playground causing little tummies to rumble. I caught a whiff of it as we stepped off the bus and walked up Oak Hill on our first ever visit to the house.

Michael and I loved it here. We were scouted out by children from the day of our very first visit. Dawn and Andrew from two doors down came up to the garden gate to ask our names as we sat on the path at the front of the house. By the time we moved in all the kids from miles around knew our names and were knocking on the front door to call for us. It wasn't long before me and Michael and our new Little Loxwood friends were out roaming and exploring this new landscape. Our territory.

Little Loxwood had an infants and a junior school on the same site with a huge playground surrounded by spacious green playing fields. At the bottom of Oak Hill there was a modern parade of shops in an L-shape. There was a butchers, a greengrocers, a chemist, an ironmongers, a post office and the news agent's which became our sweetshop. In the corner of the L was a fish and chip shop and on the end was a

21

barber's shop. Around the corner from these on a small island of grass and shrubs was a distinctive newly built circular pub constructed around a living tree, called 'The Woodsman'. Our Daddy's pub.

Mrs Price, whoever, she may be, had been quite correct, the Chapel was welcoming and I soon joined their Brownie Pack and sometimes went to Sunday School. There was the swing park and the wood park. Our parks. The swing park was by the river and the railway line and the wood park was near our house and well, in the woods. The Loxwoods, I suppose.

What a paradise for us children! We were outside daily staking our claim to our new world. My eyes always on Michael making sure he didn't get into any trouble and always making sure we were home in time for tea.

"Is that a new hole in your jeans Michael or was it already there?" I don't know why I asked. It's not as though he was going to reply. But Michael did seem to be happy in his new environment. He looked at me more often and would sometimes nod or shake his head even if he still rarely spoke.

Loxwood changed everything. It was a public housing innovation that had, in all likelihood. won awards for civil servant men in terylene suits at boozy awards dinners at Country Club hotels. Prince Charles might quite like to take a bulldozer to it but my mum, Julie, loved it. She loved the new town development and she loved the new house. She was in seventh heaven.

So in the Spring of 1975 Brian and Julie Reid and their 2.4 children – Samantha Jayne and Michael James moved into 11, Sycamore Drive, Little Loxwood. "Our first proper family home" Mummy said, "With a front, side AND back garden and nice neighbours and a fresh start."

It did feel like that for a while, it really did. The paint smelt fresh, the gas fire was warm but then before too long everything went back to being the same.

CHAPTER THREE

Mummy quickly set about turning the house into a home. She had an eye for home décor and embraced the arts and craftiness of the time. She adored making hanging pots out of bits of rope for gangly spider plants to sprawl from in our hallway window.

"This is not the hot house in Kew bloody Gardens you know Julie." Daddy moaned but he was too lazy to move them.

She delighted in collecting little herb and spice containers, designing homely little labels for them and arranging them on a miniature kitchen shelf, she had painted and put up herself.

"It's like Fanny Craddock's boudoir in here." Daddy mocked, but again, left her to it.

Mummy made friends very quickly because she was warm and lovely and kind. But Daddy's moods were as dark as the wallpaper and more unpredictable than the swirly carpet. Still he found his niche in The Woodsman and fitted in with all the other boozers who welcomed one of their own.

As his children Michael and I kept our heads down, out of range of his firing line. Though we often caught a stray bullet and occasionally a few well aimed strikes as well.

We knew things could turn nasty quite quickly like the time I was trying to teach Michael how to play Jacks. He loved any ball games and was dextrous even when quite young.

"You're really getting the hang of this." I praised him. "Try and see if you can pick six up at once this time." His hands were, of course, smaller than mine and he looked disappointed when he couldn't pick up as many as me. We were sat on the garden path absorbed as he persevered. We didn't hear Daddy come up the front steps and onto the path and even if we had we wouldn't have predicted the kick he aimed at

Michael as he walked past us towards the front door of the new house.

"Toughen up lad, sitting there playing girls games. Bloody sissy boy." Daddy snarled spitefully. Michael snivelled but didn't cry and luckily Daddy was drunk and his aim had not been so good that evening so he wasn't hurt all that much. I put the jacks and the little ball back in their small drawstring bag and took him down the wood park out of the way for a while. We were practised at cautious avoidance.

We had some nice toys which we played with and loved but we were properly poor when we first moved there, though us children hadn't really realised before. Until we moved to Little Loxwood we hadn't had so many other families to compare ourselves with. In fact, we had few possessions of any type and it only took one small van to move us all in.

But the new house was warm, downstairs anyway. There were no ants in the pantry or mice darting under the back door in and out of the kitchen. Mummys' optimism and hope was palpable. She deserved a straw to clutch at. A prospect of a brighter future.

And for me and Michael it was glorious to have a little bedroom each when previously we had shared a bed after he had grown out of his little cot. Our bedrooms were like a sanctuary for each of us and they were the only rooms in the house that were not predominantly brown, mine being orange and pink and Michaels blue and red. Mummy had decorated them and added flourishes and embellishment for it was she who did all the work around the house.

"Orange and pink for Spangle, like fizzy pop." Mum smiled at me, proud of her handiwork. She gave me a kiss as she threw the dazzling new bedspread across the bed. She had bought the gaudy thing from her catalogue, which was an important source of income for her as well as a way of being able to buy nice things she could otherwise not afford. In no time several of our close neighbours had made orders and taken accounts with her and she kept organised records in a little blue Littlewoods folder she kept in her knitting bag, diligently earning commission on all her sales. My room was very tidy because it had a built-in cupboard for my clothes and toys so most of my things were kept out of sight. Except, that is, for a ragdoll pyjama case that sat on my pillow, a little bookcase of my favourite, mostly Enid Blyton books on my bedside cabinet and a small wooden shelf above my bed which was made out of two interlocking squares and on which sat my collection of tiny glass animals. They had belonged to Aunty Cathy when she was a girl but now she lived in digs and had nowhere to keep them safe she had passed them on to me. They were very fragile so I hardly ever touched them but they did look very pretty on the little shelf. It was a lovely room with a huge window that I loved to gaze at the sky through whilst lying in my very own single bed looking at the shapes in the clouds as they drifted by.

The bedroom window had been smaller and not in my site line when we had lived in the pink bungalow. Then I had shared a bedroom and a lumpy old bed with Nanna. Listening to her grisly snoring, whilst trying not to be frightened by the sight of her grey wig on its stand on the bedside table, next to her false teeth in their little tooth bath, had been my nightly torment.

But now my lovely little girls' bedroom faced our back garden and the back gardens of the houses behind us. Sometimes on an evening I liked to keep my light off and look in at those families who hadn't closed their curtains yet. Somehow in the gentle early evening light everything seemed to me to be more golden and happy in their houses.

Because we were the end of a terrace we had our front door on the side of the house which made it different from all the others on Sycamore Drive who had their front doors on, well the front. If you opened Michaels' bedroom window you were a few feet above the reinforced glass roof of the porch that jutted out offering protection over the front door below. This was held up by a fancy white metal frame. To us this seemed luxurious shelter and it was often a play space on drizzly afternoons and a climbing frame on drier ones.

Michael and I never really strayed all that far in our skinny ribbed tops and flares. Even in our roaming packs of 'kids' we understood the boundaries. "Last one to the ladybird bushes is a monkey!" We had our invisible lines we would not cross. We knew our place.

I know that I knew mine. I knew what time to get up, I knew to make packed lunches for me and my little brother and I knew to walk us both over the road and around the green to get us to school on time. I knew the jobs I'd get into trouble for if I failed to do them and I knew what time to be in for tea and to be out of the way with Michael when my Daddy got back from the pub.

Children were second class citizens in those days. We had to make our own entertainment and stick together. Safety in numbers. If we could be seen but not heard indoors, we could make as much noise as we liked outside and that's where we usually were, rain or shine, but usually rain. Outside and inside were as different as two worlds could be. Outdoors was laughter and happiness in our gang of Little Loxwood children.

CHAPTER FOUR

It sounds strange these days but we really did call ourselves a gang. We were just little kids, growing up most of the time with our significant adults oblivious to our existence. We were always outdoors, outside the woodchip environs of home in the real woods, in the real trees, hanging upside down from our ankles.

Adults were perpetually grumpy to kids. But then they had a lot on their minds in those days. There was the cost of living and all the browness to contend with. That's why everyone smoked so many fags, it wasn't just for the coupons.

Perhaps because the landscape was dark and sad inside our nice modern house I felt I had to offer some kind of light. Not the bright morning sunlight like my Mummy. But a tiny shimmer. A spangle, as my Daddy had always called me. He liked to give people nicknames and he liked the sweets, a pack of which was always in his coat pocket. I was lucky because most of his nicknames were unkind.

So I would do things to cheer everyone up. Make a cup of tea for Mummy if she was tired. Read to Daddy from a grown-up book if he was grumpy. For some reason this impressed and pleased him very much. Distract Michael if he was being naughty to prevent him from getting a telling off or worse. Recite a poem or a hymn off by heart for Nanna.

After the first very snowy winter and Christmas in our new house, emerged a green and verdant spring. The gang breathed in the fresh air from our environs as we whooped and savoured our comradeship out of doors. We built dens and played and let the grownups deal with the worries of the world.

The changing of the seasons felt tactile because being outside we were so close to them. Spring had its own scents and flavours. The wild garlic took over huge swathes of woodland floor and crocus and daffodils on the green gave off a faint honey aroma. Birdsong became more audible and the river at the swing park started to tremble with insect life.

As the Spring stretched into Summer it took a while for the adults and the children to recognise and then to begin to enjoy the blessed phenomenon which was surreptitiously creeping up on us. As the days got steadily longer they also became warmer. A lot warmer! Cloud cover dissipated and the sun shone gloriously as the sky reigned down an incredible munificence. Pleasantly and gradually the days expanded and stretched languorously.

Then the heavens blessed us with a promise. A sun kiss.

We all shed our brown clothes and colour re-entered our drab lives.

The sun boldly shimmered. It was beautiful. Foreign. Dangerous. Dire warnings of droughts, pavements cracking. A once in a lifetime event. The summer of 76, the summer that went on for ever. And ever. And ever.

I wore hot pants and smock tops that Nanna embroidered flowers on. My hair bleached blonder in the sun. When I took my Scholls off to do a cartwheel I burnt the soles of my feet on the pavement and squealed with delight at it. Occasionally, on weekends we caught trains with our mother to places that were a very long hot walk to a busy, litter strewn beach or a packed public lido. We ate sandwiches made with sandwich spread that slithered in the intense heat on the Mothers Pride white bread and we enjoyed it. My skin was golden. I looked like sunshine and so did Michael.

Space hoppers went a bit melty. The ice cream man was overly happy and gave us free tiptops when our mothers sent us across the road to buy peacock coloured packs of ten number six from his van.

We cavorted in dazzling, hot, hot days of flying ants and washing up bottle water fights. Playing out late, because it never got dark or cold.

One sultry afternoon me, Tammy, Dawn and a girl called Jackie Jackson who lived on the other side of the main road that we weren't allowed to cross on our own were talking about the Bank Holiday Scout & Guide Gang show outside the front of my house whilst we played. Jackie's hair was wet as she had been in her paddling pool. It was so hot and looking at her made me wish we had a paddling pool as well. My Mummy said there was no point in having one because there were going to be water shortages soon if people weren't careful and carried on wasting water and then where would we all be?

We had clackers. School was thinking about whether or not to ban them because it had been on the television news that they were dangerous. They had sent a note home saying as much.

"Well they better not ban them" said Dawn "because my Mum says she will be straight down that school if they do because it's not up them what parents buy for their own kids."

Clack, clack, clack

"She says it's only a bit of fun and no one tells her what she can and cannot buy." Clack

"I wish I had pink ones and not just plain white ones" said Tammy. "Sarah Hutchinson has got day glo ones"

I was glad to have a pair at all even though they bruised my knuckles. They weren't easy to control but they had a reassuring heaviness. I was getting better at mastering them and I loved the sound- clack clack clack. Steady repetition.

"Someone in London got themselves killed with theirs and that's why they are banning them." lied Dawn. At that very moment Tammy's spun from her fingers and clacked loudly and somewhat wildly across the path and as Dawn turned her head to look in alarm her own pair flicked back towards her face hitting her and giving her an almost instant black eye.

She wasn't allowed to play clackers after that so the next evening when we were all out to play we went back to bouncing as many balls as we could control against the garage walls instead.

The sun was dropping low in the sky and there were about ten of us kids still out in the street. The honeysuckle cast its sweet fragrance from Aunty Doreen's garden which was next to the row of garages and entwinned with her hedge. Michael and Phillip had somehow climbed up onto the garages precarious grooved rooves. The bouncing balls were quite noisy and we sung special songs that went along with the game. We would make sure we tried to aim the tennis balls at the No Ball Games Allowed sign and hit it as many times as we could. So when Michael fell off the roof and quietly landed in a twisted clump on the floor I didn't notice to begin with even though he was only a few yards away from my own feet on the gritty tarmac in front of the garages.

Then Tammy did and she poked me hard. My hands lost control, balls were dropped, bouncing quietly down into the gutter, collecting there on the metal grid. I stared at him. He was not crying and his eyes were open but he was very still and clearly unable to move. And as the gang drew a collective gasp, and the ripple of panic spread through all of us neither could I. Dawn was stood next to me and she held my hand.

I could not take my eyes off him I was paralysed. Someone else, Gary or Phillip must have run to our house. I just stood there staring at Michael. I was trembling. My brother was probably dead, he looked dead. My Daddy would kill me, he was going to shout and swear and wave his arms, he would be crashing around the furniture and I wouldn't know when and if he was going to hit me. He would blame me because it was all my fault and then he would blame Mummy and then…… a neighbour, Uncle Tom from number 13, came rushing over, he picked Michael up and put him and Mummy in his car and he drove them to the hospital.

His wife, a woman we called Aunty Beryl, but who of course was no relation to any of us, gently took me into her house.

Aunty Beryl was kind and I had been in her house before. She had sponsored me for something and given us sweets on Halloween. Aunty Beryl had a kid that was too old to be in our gang. She was called Karen and had a job at the paper shop and she gave us sweets sometimes. Flying saucers. She was a little bit fat and she had a twinkly smile and I now realise that she had Down's syndrome. Karen had a little Yorkshire terrier dog so the house smelled of it. Aunty Beryl put a blanket around me and made me a cup of very sweet tea.

They had a colour telly and it was on but I was too afraid to look at it. I was shaking badly, and I felt cold even though the evening was still very warm. I was too upset to cry or move or do anything other than sit there on their velveteen sofa until I eventually fell asleep still sitting upright.

My Mummy came after what felt like a very long time and she picked me up in the blanket and carried me home across the road. The sky was navy black and the moon and the stars bright. The night air tasted fresh and tart. Mummy carried me calmly and gently. She whispered as we went into our house and she showed me that my little brother was fast asleep in bed, snug and contented. He had a bandage around his head. He was cuddling his teddy. He looked so peaceful and sweet. He was even snoring quietly in the moonlight from his open window.

Then Mummy put me in my bed without making me clean my teeth or wash my face or say my prayers. But I said them in my mind anyway. I knew I had to thank God because my Daddy wasn't in the house. He was out somewhere. He didn't know anything about any of it. My brother needed rest but he was going to be fine Mummy said. Nothing broken, minor concussion.

So Daddy had nothing to get angry about, he didn't even know that Michael had climbed on the garages, or that I hadn't been looking after him properly or that he had been to hospital in a neighbour's car. Even if he noticed Michael had a mark or a bandage we could make it seem like something less serious. Now that everything was alright and Daddy himself didn't look bad and wasn't personally affected in any way or expected to do anything about it he wouldn't even care. We had got away with it, Daddy need never know the horror of that evening.

Finally lying safely in my bed in my luminescent orange and pink room I did feel a relief. Though the tension didn't completely leave my body, I was no longer rigid and I could make small movements. I scrunched my eyes and put my hands together and said in my head- Thank you, thank you God. Thank you.

Mummy came back in to check on me before going to bed herself. She tucked me in, smoothed down my hair and she told me she loved me before kissing me calmly goodnight. She smiled and I read relief on her face too.

Everything was alright.

Making a wobbly jelly in the shape of a rabbit usually cheered up everybody. I was helpful and sunny whenever I could be. I kept my bedroom tidy and sometimes tidied Michaels toys away for him in his. I would run down to the shops for my parents if they had forgotten something and go over to Uncle Ed's to ask if we could borrow a screw driver or a drill or whatever it was Dad might need to borrow to attempt to fix something.

I could usually make my Daddy smile if I put some effort into it and I would do so if I thought it could diffuse a bad situation.

I was popular with the neighbourhood girls and they magnanimously let me play with their nice toys and I would let them play with my hair. They loved brushing it, plaiting it, wrapping it around my head.

"You're like a living Sindy." Dawn said one afternoon, weaving a chain of daisies around a bun she had fashioned on the crown of my head.

Little Loxwood was the friendliest place we had ever lived and I remember feeling a small but burgeoning sense of belonging. I remember it tangibly, like it was a thing.

Me, and my two closest friends, Dawn and Tammy would sit on the wall of my side garden loudly singing our favourite chart songs together. Even at that young age we had discernment and a sense of what was good music, what constituted dire music and what was silly and jokey but maybe worth a sing a long anyway like 'Combine Harvester' by the Wurzels or 'Jeans On' by David Dundas.

Our trio could belt out a powerful rendition of 'Leader of the Pack' complete with background motorbike revving sound effects! And any passer-by would tell you that our version of 'Young Hearts Run Free' was particularly heartfelt. I still know all the words to this day. "Never be hung up, strung up like my man and me" we crooned in our fake American singing voices.

School was a different world, separate from everything. A portal to other dimensions. At juniors, doing a project about Loxwood through the ages I remember not believing that these things I learnt about Roman villas and coins, the derelict millhouse and the corn laws and the wild emboldened Chartists could be anything to do with this very contemporary place in which we had come to live.

Sometime during the school year that I became 8 years old I was made class 'monitoress'. (Only boys could be actual monitors back then.) My main duty was to take the register back to the office after we had all been marked in. I liked doing this. The register was important and I stood behind 'Miss' as she called out the names and made her marks in it. Then she would blot the ink with a long strip of blotting paper and hand it to me with a smile. Sometimes I also got to give out pencils, sharpeners and rulers. It was all quite a power rush for a little girl of my age.

Michael and I would arrive at the school crossing each morning together and wait on the kerb for the lollipop lady before we crossed. Some cheeky kids would step out. But we waited properly like Mummy had taught us.

Once on the school side of the road I would give Michael his Tupperware with his lunch inside, say "Goodbye, be good" and then go about my school day without seeing or speaking to him again until home time. The infants, though on the same site, was quite separate from the juniors. I had no idea what he did in there each day. I had my own life.

My classroom was a glass box of lovely smells, sights and sounds. There were windows down each side, the front ones facing the playground outside and the ones to the left of the blackboard peered into the main corridor of the building. Mrs Goodchild controlled this domain and every little thing that went on within it. She knew the whereabouts of every pair of scissors and exactly how many pieces of chalk were at her disposal. Mrs Goodchild held all our daily actions in her wise consideration.

"Please Miss can I go to the toilet please?"

"It's ten minutes to playtime. I think you can wait another ten minutes."

Some bolder children might risk imploring her, "Please Mrs Goodchild I'm desperate." and she would shake her head

35

sternly and sadly at these. I would never have been that audacious, I would rather suffer until my bladder ruptured. I was one of the children who kept their heads down and attempted, despite a faint aspiration to occasional praise, to achieve invisibility.

For me school was a heady blend of happiness and confusion. Awkwardness and enjoyment. It was noisy and industrious. But it was safe and reassuring too. I loved the books, the sugar paper, glue pots and the smell of chalk dust. I did love to learn, especially reading. I was particularly good at recitation which was big in my school in those days. This is basically learning poems off by heart and saying them out loud as if you were acting out the story. 'The Lady of Shallot' was my speciality and I would do a special mime with my hands in front of my face when –'the mirror cracked, from side to side.' Inside I would be mortified with embarrassment each time I did this but loved it at the same time.

We sang a lot (hymns), communally said the Lord's Prayer daily and slotted all the Christian religious festivals into the currents of the seasons and the school calendar year. The whole school said grace collectively before dinner (lunch) - "For what we are about to receive, may the Lord make us truly thankful. Amen." And I, for one, was because I wasn't having to eat school dinners that looked to me like gruel and cold cabbage as I was a 'sandwiches' kid.

Christmas at school was huge and it was the one time the infants came in through the adjoining door to our hall and took part in a joint production. We put on a wooden but colourful nativity play creaky enough to put a tear in our mother's eyes (Fathers never came into schools then unless there was something very wrong). It was a taste of performance and every child had a special part to play.

"You're the best shepherd I've ever seen Michael." Mummy said to my brother still clad in his dressing gown with a tea towel tied onto the top of his head with an old tie. He was too terrified to respond in any way, paralysed by shyness because Juniors was another planet and he was out of his usual orbit.

Enthusiastic teachers and children decorated the school to within an inch of its institutional functionality. Father Christmas actually came in on his sleigh to talk to us and to tell us to be good children then give us each a colourful notebook as a present. In the very last few days of the Christmas term things would relax a little we were allowed to bring in books to read and games to play. As a treat we would get to watch Norman Wisdom or St Trinian's films in the Hall on a big screen projector. Then we would have Christmas dinner and even the 'sandwiches' children would get a mince pie and a drink of squash.

Being introduced to the world of St Trinians fired up my imagination and I dreamed of going to a boarding school just like that. If I went there or somewhere like there I thought I would even stay there in the holidays and never come home because that school looked so wonderful. With its criminal gangs of jauntily dressed girls, free and feisty living in charming, dilapidated debauchery. Not much like Little Loxwood Juniors, though I think they had the same nasty milk as us and the teachers all smoked.

CHAPTER SIX

Suddenly school broke up for the summer holidays and we were outside on the streets more than ever. Our best prank was the 'rope'. There were fewer cars on the roads and not many parked cars either so visibility for drivers and children playing in the street was good. Half the kids in our 'gang' would position themselves on the pavement on one side of the road with the other half stood on the pavement directly opposite – approximately six a side with a single kid at the street entrance a few yards up ahead. For a driver turning into our road this was already likely to be an intimidating sight despite the fact that we were all under 10 years old. The kid keeping watch would have called out "CC" to the rest of us. This was our secret cunning code for car coming and would be the signal for us all to start silently counting- 1,2,3,4,5. On 5 the lead child on each side stooped to the kerb. Then they would slowly mime picking up a rope and we would all assume a tug of war position behind them, stretching back a taunt, tight imaginary barrier across the road in the warm duskily lit evening.

The leaders would be making sure they were looking directly at the driver and that he had seen them (not many women drove in those days). Uncertainty, confusion flashing across the drivers face.

The car would inevitably do an emergency stop and brake abruptly at which point we would all scatter and run laughing around the block to the green, which thanks to new town planners, cars could not access.

We would all be hysterically laughing, on a high, describing the drivers' facial expressions and working out whose dad it may have been (not mine, we couldn't afford a car).

After about fifteen minutes we would be back on the street doing it all over again or playing bulldog or standing in a line on our side garden wall taking it in turns to pretend to shoot each other. The best death wins. A summer daze of camaraderie and happiness.

The numbers of kids out each day and evening fluctuated. The summer holidays drifted along lazily and once school broke up some kids went away on a holiday or disappeared off with their families on day trips. Sometimes children weren't allowed out for a few days for some misdemeanour. But most days when we were out roaming there could be any number between 6 and sixteen of us in our Sycamore gang. This mainly included kids who actually lived on the same road as us but some lived around the corner on Larch Road and a few around the back green on Chestnut Close. The gang consisted of big kids and littler kids but no very big kids. Juniors and Infants only. There were no formal rules but you knew if you belonged or not. The really big kids from the big school at Crossridge would have had no interest in us and the ones of us approaching 11 would be starting to worry about going there and the impending loss of status that was currently enjoyed both at school and in the gang.

So whilst things indoors may have remained sludge brown and oatmeal, outside children were turning shades of honey, bronze and umber. That heatwave unleashed something that was almost as good as the concept of going to St Trinians. Children were liberated by the warmth and by being outdoors more than ever. We were creating our own worlds, glorious realms of freedom.

The weather was intoxicating and liberating. Even the grown-ups started to slowly make their way outside venturing a few steps closer to our world. They became more relaxed and a bit more colourful and noticeable themselves. They sat outside in front gardens chatting unguardedly. They smoked and drank together in front of us whilst we got up to the usual mischief and sometimes one or two might even get up and join in with a game of rounders or bulldog for a laugh. They said things in front of us as though we didn't have ears or comprehension and some of us noticed things and saw things we hadn't seen before.

For example, a few days into the summer holidays I noticed my dad starting to act a bit nicer to my mum. I then noticed him trying to be a bit kinder to Michael and to attempt to look, in public at least, like a good father. It was clearly an effort for him but he tried not to goad Michael or call him a 'nancy boy' or a 'bloody pouf' if he cried when he hurt himself or if he went to kiss Daddy goodbye. He also occasionally passed a ball at him at a pace that gave Michael an opportunity to be able to successfully kick it back.

In the street Dad went out of his way to look playful and funny and to interact with us in a way that was less frightening than it was behind closed doors. I found this even more worrying than the usual version of him but my little brother, desperate for warmth, well he took the bait. His usually downturned golden head tilted upward more, his sweet childish cherry lips spoke a little more and even smiled occasionally and then I started to notice that he sometimes laughed and started to show off more in the gang. He became emboldened and climbed ever higher up in the trees and he leapt from the higher garden walls.

"Look at your brother!" called Tammy "He's right at the top of that tree." She giggled nervously as she pointed him out. He was as agile as a small ape as he laughed and threw sticks down at us from the heights of the oak on the verge at the side of our garden.

Then my Dad didn't come home for a few days and Mum said he had gone to Nannas 'for a break'. When he came back he was even nicer to us but there was a chill between him and Mum.

"Cheer up Juliette, your Romeo has returned!" It had been nice not having to dodge his moods for a short time and he

40

had bought us all presents, an Enid Blyton book for me (Mallory Towers!!! A whole new boarding school world to discover), a matchbox car for my brother and a box of Milk Tray for Mummy so I couldn't see the problem. In fact, I made a mental note to myself to start asking God in my night-time prayers if Daddy could go away more often.

Michael and I usually ate at the breakfast bar in the kitchen but tonight Mummy put the sausages and mash down on the big dinning table at the top end of the living room and we all ate together with Daddy at the head of the table with his focus set firmly on Nationwide on the black and white TV at the far end of the room.

"Can we watch Z Cars tonight Dad?" asked Michael audaciously.

"No" snapped Mum, "It's not a programme that is suitable for children"

"Of course they can Julie, it's the school holidays let them stay up late tonight with Dad the Bad. Be nice to all watch something together. Cops and Robbers, bang bang eh Michael?"

Mum didn't know whether to be cross with him for undermining her or pleased because he wanted to be nice to us so she silently went out to the kitchen with the dishes to wash up. Then she poked her head through the hatch and said "Only if you wash, clean your teeth and put your pyjamas and nightie on."

"Chip chop" said Dad to me and Michael smiling his Jimmy Tarbuck gap tooth smile. Mum put a beer down in front of him and then lit up a fag. By the time we came back down Mummy had finished clearing up.

Michael wanted to sit on Dad's lap but Dad pushed him off and called him a baby so he curled up next to me on the leatherette mustard brown sofa. Dad had his own chair and if he was in the house no one else was allowed to sit in it. It was right next to the gas fire and had the best line of sight to the telly. There was a synthetic crazily patterned rug in front of the fireplace on top of which was Dads' matching leatherette pouffee for him to perch his cheesy feet on, usually in the fire's warmth though tonight there was no need for that.

"Please put your slippers on Brian so we don't all have to breathe in that aroma!" Mummy said snobbily and even Daddy laughed and did as he was told as we all watched Stratford John swearing and nicking baddies in a monochrome glow.

Mum passed around her box of chocolates and Michael took ages to pick his choice. Dad downed his beer quickly and Mummy provided another one, he soon passed out in his chair and started to snore so Mum took us off to bed before the finish despite Michael's complaining. She tucked us in and told us she loved us, "Don't forget to say your prayers Spangle." She said kissing my forehead. As if I would.

CHAPTER SEVEN

Me, Tammy and Dawn were in the Brownies. The whole concept of the Brownies was totally thrilling, everything was wonderful in Brownies and the uniforms were the icing on the cake. Smart brown, of course, cotton little costumes with belts, neckerchiefs, sashes and berets. We were in packs, like wolves - I was in the Imps, Tammy was a Pixie and Dawn was an Elf. There were other packs too but I only properly remember ours. We marched, we sang and we did activities. We promised to serve the Queen and help other people and to keep the Brownie Guide law. We loved it.

You got badges to sew on your arm for doing things like carving a rose out of a bar of soap with a blunt pen knife.

I gave the soap rose that earnt me my Handicrafts Badge to my Mummy for a birthday present, "Thank you Spangle. Homemade gifts are made with love. This is very special."

I also had another badge, called the Hospitality Badge. A neat brown triangle with a yellow cup of tea embroidered on it which I got for making and taking a cup of tea and a fairy cake across the road to an old lady that lived in the flats by the ladybird bushes. Making the tea and cake was the easy bit. Carrying it on a little tray topped with a doily down the path, down the front steps, across the road and into the ladies flat without spilling it was more of a challenge. I am sure the tea was tepid by the time I proudly handed it to her, dressed in my uniform but she had the good grace to drink it and sign my handbook for me to prove that I had completed the task and had earned my badge.

At the moment though, Brownies was even more exciting than usual. Meetings were a hive of activity and excitement as we were practising singing, dancing and acting out sketches. This was because on the August Bank Holiday we were going to be putting on something called a Gang Show which we were doing with the Guides, the Cubs and the Scouts. All the Brownies were going to be in it and your whole family could come and watch you. Nanna and Aunty Cathy were going to come. Nanna was in the process of making me a special sailor dress to wear in one of the routines. It was navy, white and red and had a big collar like a sailors' bib.

The show had a nautical theme and I was learning the words to 'On the good ship lollipop' which was going to be the penultimate song and dance routine and the climax to the show. My Mum was going to have to put rags in my hair so that I would have ringlets like someone called Shirley Temple who had once sung the song in a film. I had to sing some lines in the middle of the song all by myself, this is called a Solo, because Brown Owl thought I looked like her, Shirley Temple. I was also going to have to do a little tap dance at the same time. The thought of this set off butterflies in my tummy.

Brown Owl and Tawny Owl were in charge of us Brownies though the Minister sometimes came into the Hall as well to see what we were doing, especially if we were making a bit of a noise. The Hall was attached to the Chapel but it was to the side of the building and felt quite separate and less religious. There were other rooms off it as well and there was a long narrow ante room with a kitchen and a counter from which food could be served and where us Brownies had squash and biscuits halfway through.

The Hall was large, airy and purpose built and in this heat the side doors were all opened wide letting in lemony early evening sunshine. It had a grand stage with steps up to it at the front. Normally we weren't allowed up there and even now with rehearsals in full swing it was only under careful supervision.

Tawny Owl was very good at playing the piano and she taught us the songs whilst clanging out the tunes on the shiny dark instrument that sat below the stage to the left of the steps. We would sit in a semi circle on the floor around her, repeating the words line by line until they were sung to her satisfaction.

The sumptuous maroon velvet curtains, which were usually closed, were open as were the safety curtains behind. Older children were industriously sawing bits of wood and painting large screens to make sets and an awful lot of work and effort was going into putting on an entertaining show for all the family.

Mummy said that my Grandma and Grampa were also going to come and watch me from all the way from the other side of the country but my Uncle Nigel and my cousins I don't know can't come because they live in Australia, which is on the other side of the world.

CHAPTER EIGHT

It was only two days later that Michael impaled his inner leg on a twisted piece of wire fencing whilst climbing into a building site with some older boys. They had been exploring. This injury was quite nasty and a lot worse than his previous head injury because it was a puncture wound and the jagged barbed had torn through muscles and ligaments deep inside his leg when he had pulled it out. It was painful. As it was the daytime and he could hobble Mummy took him to the hospital on the bus. He was welcomed as the returning hero, some of the nurses on duty having remembered him from the other night. They made a big fuss of him because he looked like a sweetly dishevelled cherub.

Whilst Mummy was getting Michael treated I stayed at Dawns house and Aunty Shirley made us egg and chips whilst we played with Dawns' Sindys and her brother Andrew's Action Men lining them all up in couples and giving them glamorous names and occupations like executive business man and window dresser. I had heard Daddy say that they had a new window dresser starting at the shop where he worked and this sounded like a very exotic thing to do to me.

Michael came home from the hospital with a wadded pad wrapped to his thigh with a thick bandage. He couldn't get his jeans on over it but as it was so very hot it was fine for him to wear shorts so that didn't matter. It was impossible to totally keep this accident from Daddy but Mummy made it sound like Michael had done something brave and manly and this helped no end and anyway Daddy was still trying to be nice to us all. If anything Daddy seemed proud of his little son's war wound.

And so Michael was the first person in the gang to ever have stitches even though he was one of the youngest. Although the hole in his flesh was quite a deep one it wasn't very long so there were only five actual stitches but these stitches made his accident a source of great interest to all the local children. People kept dropping by and he had to show all the aunties and uncles even though the mark was only a tiny reddish black lumpy line of clotted blood and thread.

He was wallowing in all the attention and neighbours kept knocking on the door with comics and sweets for him. Of course, he even had his own bottle of radioactive looking Lucozade wrapped in its crinkly orange plastic cellophane that the lady from the chemist on the parade bought up. He was being completely spoilt, for being naughty. It was quite ridiculous really, or so I thought. Lots of the kids in our gang had made him get well cards. Michael had an angelic look and was smaller than most six year olds and for some reason people seemed to feel sorry for us.

Because of this tidal wave of kindness and care though, my Daddy felt he had to buy some kind of gift for his heroic young son too. So Daddy being Daddy, he randomly bought Michael a swing ball set. This was new out and was being heavily promoted in the shop he worked in. There was even one set up as part of a summer display in one of the main windows, presumably by a window dresser. But it was really an adult or at least a teenagers game. It was very much too big for Michael and stupidly expensive but it was a present. It was metallic, spikey and dangerous looking and I personally did not think it was a good present, though I was not stupid enough to say as much. We all smiled as they faffed around getting it out of the box. Michael was pleased and protective of it and said how great it was even though he had really wanted new skates. "Alright sonny Jim?" said Daddy ruffling Michael's hair. "We'll have a game of that when you're better. Just nipping down the pub Julie. The boys 'll be waiting for me. Big darts match tonight".

"Thanks Dad, hope you win" Michael smiled.

"Good lad." Dad returned, rushing out as fast as he could, but bestowing on his son a smile and a wink as he went past.

47

Nobody in our family mentioned this change in Daddy. Perhaps they put it down the perpetual sunshine. He wasn't fooling me though, I knew what he was really like. I knew there had to be some ulterior reason for this rush of awkward kindness.

Mum enjoyed nursing him and Michael recovered in no time. Us kids drifted back outside and it was hot, so hot. One afternoon Dad came home from work in the car of a friend of his from work. He was sweaty and excited, over dressed for the sultry weather in his work suit.

"Juliette love. Julie, Come out here." He called out to Mummy from the path.

There was something half in and half out of the man's boot. A huge cardboard box. Dad said he had had a pay rise and so he had bought us a fridge with a little freezer bit at the top. He looked so pleased with himself. It had taken a heatwave for our family to have our first ever fridge.

"What do you think of that then Julie, girl?" Mummy was besides herself. All the neighbours could see it coming up the front path.

"Cashed in all your Greenshield stamps then have you Brian?" smirked Aunty Shirley from a stripey deckchair on her front lawn. He ignored her as he and his friend struggled in the heat to bring it into the house.

There was a fridge sized gap in our kitchen where Mummy kept her laundry basket and she quickly moved this so they could slip the white Fridgidare in. I took the milk and the butter off the slab and out of our built-in pantry and placed them in the new contraption and then messed about with the little light. Yup, a real fridge like the ones in other people's houses. Mum found some squash and we made ice lollies in tupperware beakers. I made a jelly!!! It was fantastic and it did look very modern in comparison to our other household appliances especially the dilapidated old twin tub.

48

Then on another hot afternoon, not long after the fridge, Dad came home from work with an inflatable paddling pool in a bag under his arm. He actually went over the road himself and borrowed Uncle Ed's car pump and pumped most of it up before he got bored and Mum finished doing it. We waited what felt like hours for it to fill up, with Uncle Ed's hose, and then we all sat in it expectantly. Unbelievably at that moment the only huge cloud of the summer drifted across the sky immersing us in a temporary shade. But this could not dampen our spirits and even Dad himself got in it for a few minutes. He benignly let Mum take a photo of all three of us, my brother beaming, me squinting and my Dad looking like the cat that had got the cream.

"Bet your friends ain't got one as good as that eh Spangle? Blue as well. Your favourite colour" he winked at me with a cock of his head. Then he got out and got dressed and went off down the pub. Then the sun came back out and we actually started to splash around and enjoy ourselves in it. Mummy ate her words and wasted valuable water topping it up with buckets carried from the sink from time to time. She got out the old beach towels and deckchairs and let some of our friends from the gang come in whilst she chatted happily to the neighbours over the fence.

I did love that paddling pool and blue really is my favourite colour. (Don't tell Mummy but I really don't like pink at all). We splashed in there for hours that afternoon and many others too that shimmering summer. Me and Dawn did handstands in it and wriggled across the slippery plastic base on our tummies like wiggly fishes laughing. We lolled about in it until the skin on our fingers and toes got wrinkly singing 'Here Comes the Sun' and we had competitions to see who could hold their breaths the longest underwater in it.

Michael and his friends loved it too. Him and Robert played with a small football for hours in there, each end being an imaginary goal. Michael had metamorphosed from a sad, thoughtful boy to a crazy little show off that summer. My Nanna came to stay with us for the weekend and she said it was "Like you've swallowed a box of springs Michael. You and your sister better come to Chapel with me tomorrow morning so I can remind you how it feels to sit still."

"Aw no Mum, do we have to?"

"Yes, give me a bit of peace to cook the Sunday dinner and Nanna needs the company."

"That's not fair."

"No. It's not fair it's market." said Nanna. What the heck was that supposed to mean? God we were really going to have to go with her?

"Please Spangle "Mum implored, "Go with her, chapel is important to her and I don't have the time."

"Do what your mother says!" barked Daddy from behind the paper in his old tone. So that was it then. We were going to chapel tomorrow, like it or not. Not, obviously.

Nearly two hours in a stone cold building was enough to dampen the spirts of any children and we were no exception. Blah blah Jesus blah said the Minister ten thousand times. When we fidgeted too much on the hard wooden pews Nanna would fish into her jacket pocket and pass us both a mint imperial each which would subdue us for a short time. I swung my legs back and forward analysing the diagonal pattern on my long white socks whilst waiting to see how fast I could stand up when it felt like we might be about to get to the next hymn. Singing was nice. I knew all the words to all the hymns and they were reassuring and strident. Michael didn't like them and sometimes he didn't even bother to get up. He sat there on the pew and picked away at a scab on his knee and looked sullen.

When the minister said the prayer, I put my own hands together and solemnly closed my eyes and looked down. Only half listening to his boring voice I said my own prayer in my head using some of his words but finishing it off with the little prayer I said in my own bed every single night before I went to sleep. I was of the mindset that it would be greedy to ask God for 'things' because I knew we should always be grateful for what we've got. Neither did I want to name anything I thought He should change or fix because that might seem like I was criticising the Almighty because he had made things as they were in the first place. So instead, in my mind with eyes still tightly closed and hands now sweatily clasped, after the ritual of thanking God for all the good things I had like my Mummy, my elephant dress, salt and vinegar crisps, Brownies and so on I said the phrase that my young mind felt best covered what I needed to ask Him for and which I ended every one of my nightly prayers with, "and please God can you make everything turn out right. Thank you God, Amen"

Nanna loved every moment of Sunday Services and was taken away to another place. Her girlhood, her wedding perhaps and a life of hard work, routine and a certainty in God. She looked very old to me in the diluted green light of the contemporary chapel. I could see bristles of grey above her lip as she sang in her quiet but purposeful voice. I don't know what she made of the modern building but the architects had done their best to make it as draughty and uncomfortable as the older chapels she had previously dragged us along to so she probably really liked it.

After the service was over Nanna wanted to stay and talk to the Minister about something. We wanted to run around. There were a handful of other kids there too and the Sunday School room around the back where children could colour in pictures of Samson and Delilah or David and Goliath was open so we wandered around there. There were big kids outside picking up the stones from the gravel walkways and throwing them at the young, newly planted trees. There was just one kid colouring that I didn't know and I was fed up now and just wanted to go home. And it was very hot. I looked around for Michael as I thought we needed to go and see if Nanna was finished. He was looking in awe at the older rough looking kids, clearly admiring them. He bent down to pick up a handful of stones but I swooped and knocked them from his hand dragging him away.

"I don't know what's got into you Michael. I really don't." He looked innocently at me for a split second then cast his head back down to its usual angle and he let me take him back round to the front of the Chapel. Nanna was smiling as she chatted to the Minister and some other old ladies and I told her we would walk on but on seeing us she came too. I wondered if they were talking about Jesus and the Disciples or about real things. Either way she was beaming and clearly happy with the way her Sunday had gone. She was especially pleased with us for coming and she reached into her ancient sagging purse and gave us a 10 penny piece each on the way home as our reward.

Dinner was ready and we all ate together at the big table in the sitting room which Mummy had laid out nicely. For once Dad didn't bully us or force feed us vegetables he knew we didn't like, as he usually would. Even Nanna was puzzled because she had previously had to witness this Sunday ordeal and had long given up trying to intervene. Daddy ate, gave praise to Mummy for the cooking and then put on his brand new suede jacket (in the blazing heat) and told us he was off to the pub. I rolled my eyes and looked at Mum. She shrugged and looked at Nanna. Michael said,

"Can I come Dad?" pushing his luck.

"No you bloody can't "said Dad "and don't leave the table till all those carrots are eaten."

"There's children in Africa who would love those carrots" said Nanna feeling she had to say something.

"Well they can have them if they want them" mumbled Michael quietly, looking at me. We smirked but thankfully Daddy was out the door and the carrots were wrapped up in a tissue and quickly flushed away down the toilet in case he came back unexpectedly.

CHAPTER NINE

After Nanna had gone back home on the bus the day erupted into another boiling hot afternoon. I was cleaning out the guinea pigs' hutch in a wedge of shade at the back of the house directly underneath the open kitchen window. Mum was in there with Aunty Beryl and Aunty Shirley smoking fags and gossiping. Herbert was a pointless creature but he was the only pet we were allowed though Michael longed for a dog.

"You're not having a bloody dog. Do you know how much it costs to feed a mutt?" end of Daddy's discussion on the matter. So after months of going and gazing at various small caged animals at the pet stall in the indoor market in town we had chosen an unattractive and uninteresting alternative that we had to share the care of. Herbert – the Reid family pet. Michael didn't mind it but I wasn't that keen on picking him up. I hated the feel of his little bones and his heartbeat as he trembled in my arms. Still I carefully placed the poor creature in a shoe box on the top of the hutch whilst I brushed out the dirty saw dust and attempted to improve his bleak living conditions.

"I don't know how you put up with it Julie." Aunty Shirley's voice drifted through the open window with the cigarette smoke.

"Sandy says he tells all the women down the pub that he's a single man whilst you sit in at home with his kids. I know it's not for me to say but...."

"That's just how he is, he's just a joker. Everyone round here knows who Brian is and that he's married. It doesn't mean anything Shirl."

"I'm sure" Aunty Beryl agreed, sounding a bit doubtful.

"Anyway," said Mummy "I don't know what any other woman would see in Brian. He's not exactly Georgie Best!" They all laughed at this witticism.

"No, but you don't want 'im taking you for granted Julie. You're a good girl and a looker too. You deserve better." Aunty Shirley persisted.

"Well a leopard doesn't change his spots so I don't see what I can do about it. For better or worse, you know that. Forever and ever, amen"

"How does he like that new job in Fosters?" My Daddy had apparently secured a better paid and higher status job in a menswear store. I don't think he had been in his previous job in the department store all that long, it seemed like he was always getting new jobs.

"I love seeing him go off every day in a suit!" collective cackles, "I think he likes it there. Says the staff in are all friendly. At least he doesn't come home moaning about it each and every day like that last place. I do appreciate the bit of extra money in my housekeeping though it's not much and it doesn't go very far. If I didn't have my catalogue and a bit extra from my Tupperware parties me and the kids wouldn't have anything to wear. He says I should get myself a part time job if I want money to spend. Brian doesn't understand the basic cost of living. He reckons I spend too much money on the children and if I was earning I'd be a bit more careful"

"Hmm well Sandy and I feel it's the man's job to provide for the family."

"O yes, so do me and Bri." Mum was feeling uncertain now and worried she had been disloyal and said too much.

I picked Herbert up out of his shoe box and put him back into his nice clean hutch. I unhooked his water bottle from the mesh of the caged bit and opened the back door to go into the kitchen to the sink to top it up.

"Hello Spangle love" said Mum. "Where's Michael?"

"He's playing with his cars upstairs" I said rinsing out the little bottle. The other ladies smiled affectionately all puffing away.

"You enjoying the school holidays Samantha? At least we can't complain about the weather." said Aunty Shirley "Uncle Sandy and me are thinking of taking our Dawn and Andrew down to the caravan next week if you'd like to come with us? What do you think Julie? "

"Um that's kind Shirl. I'll have to talk to Brian. Would you like that love?" Mum asked me. I shrugged. I didn't know if I would like that. Though I would have liked to see the inside of a caravan and even stay in one, one day. Caravans were like toy houses. Dawn's Sindy doll had one and they did look wonderful with everything smaller than at home and tidied cleverly away out of sight.

"A free week at the seaside. Do you a world of good Sam and give you a bit of a break too Julie."

"I'll speak to Brian and let you know." Mum said. I went back outside with Herbert's water. I hated being called Sam. Could I put up with that for a week? Dawn was alright but I wasn't that keen on her brother Andrew. A week sounded like a long time away from home.

After they had gone back to their own houses Mum asked me again if I wanted to go. Michael wasn't invited and she thought it might be nice for me to have a break from him. But I was worried about who would look after him without me there. I didn't feel comfortable with the idea but I could see Mum thought it was too good an offer to refuse.

I needn't have worried about it though because when Dad came back from the pub he was the wrong side of drunk and he took it as a personal insult when Mum mentioned the invitation.

"We don't need their bloody charity." He snarled nastily at her.

"Well it's not like we can afford to take the kids anywhere ourselves is it Brian?" Big mistake.

"What do you mean by that you bloody bitch?" Armchair awkwardly pushed back as he tries to stand up furiously. His balance is wrong and his right arm raised slightly. My stomach knots.

"Nothing Brian. Just would be nice if we could afford a little holiday one day. Maybe next year now you've got this new job eh?" Though she said this calmly I could see Mummy was trembling and so was I and my tummy felt funny. Michael kept very still with his long white hair in his eyes, hardly breathing.

My Daddy digested what Mummy had said. There was a long silence as he stood over us all, his arm still raised a few inches. He was a horrible purple colour and the hair on his hairline was wet and sticking to his skin. I could smell the alcohol seeping through his pores. He looked at Mummy and then at me and then across to Michael. Then breathed out loudly, like a sigh.

"Yeah, that's right." He slurred. "Next year. Next year we'll all be off to bloody Majorca. Sunny Spain. El Viva Espania. No bloody caravan in Swanage for us." He seemed to suddenly realise that he was swaying. He sat back down heavily. He was sweating a lot and he looked puffy and exhausted. "Sunny Spain!" Then he fell silent.

"Right kids" Mummy said, seizing the moment. "Dave Allen's coming on in five minutes so it's time for your bed. Say goodnight to your father." She took us each by the hand.

"Night Dad" we each mumbled quietly and giving his chair a wide berth.

"Not going to give your dad a goodnight kiss?" Daddy slurred. Michael went over and tried to hug him but Dad tousled his hair roughly and pushed him away.

"Bloody girl! Boys don't kiss boys" he snapped. His eyes were narrow and he was still very red in the face. I pecked his forehead lightly. He looked at me questioningly. Then asked, "You don't want to stay in a grotty caravan in Dorset with Sandy Pandy and Shirley Wurley anyway do you Spangle? Much rather be here with all your friends and Michael."

"Yes Dad."

"That's what I thought. Night then. Turn the box on Julie girl. Chip chop"

CHAPTER TEN

The next day super hot. Mummy used the dirty washing up water from our breakfast dishes to water the flowers in the border in the back garden. The ground beneath the grass was dry and cracked. The day was very still and had heated up early with shimmering heat already bouncing off the pavements and roads.

Eight of us kids walked down to the boating lake which wasn't that far from the parade of shops on the other side of the wood park. It was only a fifteen-minute walk but we were sweating by the time we got there. The lake glittered so brightly it was hard to look at it as it reflected the sun. There were lawns and trees all around it's gently lapping banks and a few yards away to the side was a car park partially hidden by well-established rhododendrons. Though obviously man-made it was quite a pretty spot.

Our ice cream man, Gino, was parked at the lake side of the car park doing the best business of his life and he shouted us a cheery - "Ciao!" The place was packed mainly with children and a sprinkling of teenagers. They were scattered around the shore on lying on towels or throwing Frisbees. The only adults were the two men who worked there and Gino. The glistening lake was a bobbing, noisy mass of kids in boats.

The system was efficient, luckily and we didn't have to wait too long on the jetty for boats to become available. Each brightly painted wooden craft was a different colour and on either side sported a large white circle in which a number was painted in black.

When they needed it for someone else and it was felt the present rowers had had it for long enough the man would call out on the megaphone – "Boat Number 15, can you come in please, your time is up."

You didn't need a life jacket and there was no requirement for an adult to be with you. Most of us older ones were proficient rowers and had spent many hours wrestling with oars and larking about in the large relatively shallow pool. We handed over our coins and went four to a boat. Straight away we had an energetic race around Swan Island which was slightly off centre to the middle of the silvery expanse. It was idyllic to be on the water in such heat and after the race was over we idled in our boats half listening to the numbers being intermittently called out and making a victory sign each time it wasn't ours. We were relaxed and languid dangling our arms and feet in the water to cool off in the incredible heat. All of us were cracking jokes and laughing. It felt like a near perfect day. I was in a boat with Phillip, Tammy and Jackie and we were the oldest ones out that day. Michael was in the other boat with one big kid called Gary and his little brother and sister, Robert and Stacey. We were all calling across to each other and decided to head over to the bank for a rest. Our numbers still hadn't been called yet and we needed some shade.

As our little vessel turned to face the bank I saw Michael in the other boat gazing in his usual melancholic way down into the water. He sat on the other side from the other two little ones so he wasn't really talking to them. Gary was doing all the work turning and moving the little boat towards the bank and Phillip was following him in ours. I wondered, as I often did when I saw Michael in this reflective pose what on earth he was thinking about. He looked sad, like someone in a painting. He didn't sense me watching him, he didn't look at me at all. As usual he was in a world of his own. As I watched he moved forward very slowly, almost imperceptibly, he lowered his head even further, eyes fixed on the water and then he leant over the side of the boat and silently slithered head first, down, down into the lake.

It happened so slowly. There was very little disturbance to the surface of the water, he had slid in like a snake, animalistic and surreal. Time became leaden and sounds muted and thickened as I watched him disappear into the aquamarine. Seconds passed and he didn't bob back up. I felt as if I had imagined it, after all it was so hot and the heat and the light were making hazy reflections and patterns and shapes. I felt hazy and vague myself. It was so hot!

Abruptly I realised Michael really had gone into the lake. It had not been some odd mirage or hallucination.

Both boats were close to the shore. I called out to Gary and saw that Robert had noticed and had started shouting too. I could swim so without thinking twice I jumped straight in. The water felt syrupy and it was hard to move in my terry towelling sun suit. I was aimlessly splashing for a few seconds until I realised I could just about stand on tip toes. Then I looked down and I could see him in the murk. He was only a few feet in front of me. I tried to stretch out and reach him.

Hysteria spreads quickly. Kids were screaming as I tried to pull Michael up by his t shirt which was slipping off his little body. I was splashing and grasping through the water with both hands. I could vaguely hear Gary and Phillip shouting for help. It seemed to me that he had been down there for ages. I was making no progress in getting a grip on him and I could feel panic flood through my own body. But Michael looked still. He looked peaceful, calm. He was hanging vertically in the water drifting gently with the water's own movement.

I thought, there must be lots and lots of little fish down there swimming around him, touching his cold skin. I could see translucent green weed fanning around his legs. But I could not pull him up. He kept slinking from my grasp.

"Help!" I shouted feebly.

My hands kept flailing in his direction but I was unable to release him from the water that held him. I bobbed under myself to try and get nearer to him but then spluttered back up quickly for air.

"Help!" I said again, half to myself, no one else could hear me. Who was I even asking for help from, was I speaking to God? Mummy, I wanted my mummy. I was ready to cry, the little ones Robert and Stacey were already crying.

I could see Michael so closely and so clearly. His hair spread in a halo in every direction around his eerily white young face. I could touch him but I couldn't get enough grip to bring him back to the surface.

Then very suddenly time returned to normal and the gurgling slow motion sounds in my ears retuned to the present tense as a man we didn't know appeared from nowhere. Fully clothed in jeans and tee shirt he waded effortlessly in up to just past his waist and leant forward into the green water and picked my brother up and carried him out of the lake. I followed behind, scrabbling up the bank to get out.

Michael looked limp and floppy and was dripping in the man's arms and on his clothing. Gary had a towel laid out ready on the grass. The man put Michael on it, turning his head to one side. Then he did something with his hands-on Michael's chest that made water come out of his mouth and after a few small splutters Michael started laughing and crying at the same time.

Then I did too and then we all did. Laughing and crying at the same time is an amazing feeling and once you start it's hard to stop. I looked at the young man who was wiping his hands in a corner of the towel. Through snot and tears and lake water I thanked him as he put another rolled up towel under my brother's head. He looked shy, embarrassed even, though he was a true hero. He said not one word but he nodded and gave me a small smile and then he strolled away shyly disappearing as quickly as he had magically appeared. Perhaps he felt odd to have unexpectedly saved a child's life. He was probably only a teenager himself but he seemed like a man to us. There can be no doubt that whoever he was he and whatever feelings he had about it he had just saved my reckless little brothers life.

Once again Michael was being treated like a conquering hero by the others. Gary patted him gently on his back as Michael lay in the sunshine curled into a little ball on his side. He looked dazed but had a stupid smile on his face.

"Are you Ok Michael? Breathe a few more times." I said. There were no visible marks of a near death experience to be seen anywhere on his person and I was relieved and horrified at the same time. Had this terrifying thing really happened at all or was it a heat induced delusional episode?

He was soaked to the skin and although it was such a hot day it was a little cooler now and his clothes must have felt cold against his skin. It was a slow walk back home with all of us feeling a little shell shocked but still talking over the details of what had happened again and again in disbelief. Michael was almost blue in the face when I got him home and his teeth were chattering. He looked like a little ghost.

I tried to explain what had happened even though I had no real explanation. Mummy calmly got his wet clothes off him, wrapped him in a blanket on the sofa and made a hot water bottle to get him warmed back up. I was wet too and tired and I didn't feel like playing out that evening so I went up and put my nightclothes on then went to bed early too. I felt dazed and unable to process what had happened. Michael was soon fast asleep and Mummy carried his light little body up to his bed.

I said a longer than usual prayer to God that night. I kept reliving those moments of trying and failing to reach Michael as I tried in vain to get to sleep in my hot little bedroom. I could still feel his cold thin arms slipping from my grasp. I could taste the water in my own nose and mouth. If that man hadn't have come along and saved him Michael could have died. What if he had died? People would have all been talking about it and it might have been on the news on the telly. Would it have been my fault because I couldn't pull him up from the green water? I thanked God for saving my little brother and I wondered if the young man had been some kind of angel.

Our washed little summer clothes hung cleanly and innocently outside my open window on the clothesline. I had drawn open the curtains for air and to gaze at the stars. As I led there I could hear Herbert rustling his straw down below. The sky was beautiful. I scanned it with my tired eyes and tried to work out whereabouts heaven was and considered whether or not I believed angels could actually come down to earth from there to help us humans in times of need. I knew Nanna believed this but until today I had thought it ridiculous, now I was not so sure.

CHAPTER ELEVEN

None of us mentioned the boating lake incident to Daddy. Michael seemed right as rain the next day and was straight out to play with Robert and the others once he had devoured his Weetabix. It was the main topic of discussion in the gang and I heard Mummy talking with Aunty Shirley about it over the fence, well over two fences because she lived next door but one. I caught just a snippet, "He frightened me half to death Shirley. He really did. He won't talk about it, he's not a child to open up about things but he's deep that boy." I didn't know what she meant by that and she stopped talking when she saw me and changed the subject to something else.

A few days later Michael trapped his head in a shed window. Uncle Ed jiggled and twisted him and got him out with just a splinter in his ear. Mummy removed it with some tweezers and washed it with boiled salted water. Again no one mentioned this event when Daddy came home from work.

Unfortunately, the day after that we weren't able to hide the huge tears in the leg of Michael's jeans after he got fiercely caught in the brambles chasing a kitten. This time Daddy did use a swear word and he shouted loudly about the cost of kids clothes these days. Then he cuffed Michael's ear and threw him a few harsh names and disappeared off to the pub. He wasn't all that worried about the nasty scratches on his son's hands and legs. I wondered what he would have said and done if he knew his young son had nearly drowned. Mummy said she wondered how he knew so much about the cost of kids clothes when he never ever bought any.

But we soon forgot all about these travails as just a few hours later that very same evening Daddy came back earlier than usual and not on foot either. We were watching Coronation Street when he pulled up directly in front of the sitting room window in the passenger seat of a mate's car, the same green one as before. He reached across his friend so he could trill a beep on the car horn to make sure we had all noticed him. The evening was still light and the window was open and we rushed over to see what was going on. He grinned his cheeky cocky smile and beckoned us all to come outside. Mummy switched the telly off and we all went out to see what the fuss was all about. Daddy's face was beaming as he got out of the car and walked around to the boot, his friend following him.

"You're all going to love this." he grinned. "Dad the Bad's done good!" None of us could disagree with him. This time Daddy had bought home the best prize of all. In fact, the ultimate!

"Don, take the weight mate. This thing weighs a ton" Daddy said to his gormless friend as they struggled up the steps along the path and into the house.

Michael and I went back into the house in front of them and stood wide eyed at the bottom of the stairs in our matching Ladybird pyjamas as the they clumsily manoeuvred an awkward large heavy box through the front door and into the house. There was sweat on both their brows. As they were both wearing their waxy synthetic work suits they looked mighty uncomfortable. Like modern day Laurel and Hardys.

But anyway they wobbled their way down the hall into the front room and set the thing down. You are not going to believe what it was - it was an actual real colour telly!!!

Michael could not contain his excitement. I have never seen him smile so brightly. He was jumping up and down on the spot so proud of his Daddy and so excited. I was excited too. Mum looked shocked. She helped move our old fashioned looking and very temperamental black and white one out of the way and me and Michael hung back as much as possible so we didn't get in the way either. This was a big operation.

We were the last of all our friends and neighbours to get a colour telly and I had long given up hope that we would ever have one. I had even started to repeat phrases Mum had used like "Colour telly is supposed to be bad for your eyes" and "everyone knows that black and white is more artistic to watch" when kids in the gang boasted about how much better Scooby Doo was in colour.

"Right, let's get this thing fired up. The Virginian will be on in a minute" Daddy clapped his hands together and gave us another of his gap-toothed smiles then he and his friend worked together, heads down to set it up. Daddy was clearly enjoying himself though Mummy seemed somewhat dumbstruck by the complete unexpectedness of this situation.

Still Daddy and Uncle Don seemed to know what they were doing as they messed around for a while with aerials and cables and things. Mummy made Horlicks and Daddy made her put a drop of something stronger in it and before all that long we were watching colour telly. It felt truly amazing. It wasn't quite as big a screen as the ones that Sarah Hutchins or Tammy Palmer's families had but it was a thing of beauty and it bought a splash of colour into our claggy living room. It felt so modern. I couldn't wait for something good to be on like Scooby-Doo or Top of the Pops. I felt that we were more like a normal family now that we had a colour telly like everyone else. The whole future now somehow looked brighter not just the moving pictures of little people in a box in the corner of our living room.

I think we all loved our Dad that evening. We forgot what he was really like. But excepting Michael, it was really only cupboard love.

CHAPTER TWELVE

"I just can't get by on what you give me Bri. I just can't. I've taken your advice and got a little part time job."

Silence. Stony look.

"Just down the chip shop on the parade, lunchtimes. Spangle can watch Michael for a few hours. They'll both be back at school in a couple of weeks"

We could all see Dad was thinking about how to react to this. But Mummy had also put some thought about the best approach to bringing up this subject and she carried on without giving him time to speak.

"You were right Brian. I need to put in a bit more for the kids. Pull my weight and not leave it all to you. We get a free fish supper on a Friday"

"Good idea Julie girl." She obviously had picked the correct strategy, "but watch that Kevin who runs the place I'm sure he fancies you. I've seen him looking at you before. You let me know if he tries any funny business." Mum smiled. She liked him saying things like this. It made her feel special to him even though almost all his actions demonstrated otherwise.

So Mum had a job and a few days later Dad changed his job again too. Now he was to be working in a small family owned department store called Hartleys and this was in the next town, Charmsford not Loxwood. He said Charmsford had more character than Loxwood and he had always wanted to have a job there. And anyway, as he was a bit of a charmer himself he said he would fit right in there. One of his colleagues from Fosters was coming to work in the same shop there with him too so he wasn't that worried about the staff or making new friends. He was going to be the soft furnishings department manager and Rita from the other shop was going to be the assistant floor manager.

"Be a fresh start" Daddy said "with good prospects. It's a promotion too Juliette." He would have to leave earlier than usual to get the bus because it was further away of course and he would get home later, often when we had already gone to bed. I couldn't tell if Mummy was pleased or not but she did say Hartley's was a respectable business and she had always liked their stock which was of a very high quality. To which Daddy replied, "and did I mention my staff discount?" and gave her a wink.

Aunty Cathy and Nanna were coming to stay over the weekend. They were going to take me and Michael to the seaside because it was so hot and Mummy and Daddy would be working and we deserved a treat for being such good children. There was mention of candy floss and crab fishing in rock pools and apart from having to give up my bedroom and sleep with Michael for the one night I was pretty pleased at the prospect of a day at the seaside. We were going on a coach trip and the Chapel had arranged it. There would be other children to play with and other old people for Nanna and Aunty Cathy to chat to about the hose pipe bans and the price of milk. Daddy gave me and Michael 50p each to spend!

We were up at the crack of dawn because the seaside is a long way away. I wore an orange sunburst cotton sundress Nanna had made and Michael was in his blue cotton shorts and a stripy T shirt. Mummy had made us packed lunches and rolled up our bathers in special terry towelling robes that you put on to change into your bathers so that nobody on the beach could see you undress. Nanna looked after the lunch but we were responsible for carrying our swimming stuff in a draw string bag each. Nanna looked after the 50 pence's.

The coach was nearly as much fun as the day on the beach. We had Corona pop in a crate! We were rarely allowed that at home. The kids were all as bubbly as the pop and were enjoying a collective sugar rush at the back of the bus. The driver had the radio on and we sang along to all our favourite pop songs loudly and happily. Michael was sat with Robert and they were looking at a picture book about racing cars. I was sat with Dawn and was letting her plait my hair in lots of tiny plaits. Someone had bought a set of pick up sticks but it didn't work as the bus was so bumpy.

Robert was sick from too much pop and Michael had a nosebleed but it all just got cleared up and soon we were on the sand running down the beach to the wavelets at the sea's edge.

It was beautiful. The sky was the boldest blue with not a cloud in it. The sea was turquoise translucence and it fizzed and tickled our toes and then danced over our bodies once we'd bravely dived in. Michael and Robert were by now fully recovered from the journey and had colourful inflated rubber rings around their little tummies and were skipping and splashing about happily. I was glad Michael had some kind of security device about his person when he was near the water but I needn't have worried that bright fine day as Michael was so happy to be at the seaside that he forgot to injure himself and he played joyfully with the other little ones like a normal six year old boy.

Me, Dawn and Tammy swam like Mermaids diving under the gentle waves, doing handstands in the water and popping up again laughing. My little plaits whipped my cheeks as I shook my head when I burst up through the sea after swimming underwater. The water was briny and refreshing and the sand beneath felt both rough and soft against the skin of our feet.

We made up sea stories and acted them out as the sun dried the salt in little white ridges on our skin. Nanna dug us a sand fort to sit and eat our sandwiches in and Aunty Cathy took a few snaps of us within it with her new camera. White teeth and sun-bronzed skin preserved by Kodak.

Whilst we enjoyed our picnic Nanna, Aunty Cathy and Aunty Beryl were talking about Daddy's new job. They all seemed pleased and very knowledgeable about this boost to my father's working status. It seems that in the local retail world getting a managerial post at Hartleys was seen as an important career move, especially by Nanna who believed the Hartley family to be a Godly one.

Tammy and Dawn had crossed over to the promenade to go to the toilets so I was eating my picnic alone whilst keeping a sharp eye on Michael who was digging for water just a few yards in front of me.

Nanna was harping on proudly about Daddy saying "I always thought Brian could go far if he applied himself. He has very good customer facing skills." I heard Aunty Cathy stifle a laugh as this uncharacteristic sentence somehow made it's way out of Nanna's lips.

"Oh yes!" said Aunty Beryl kindly. "Brian can be very personable."

"His new boss told him he hired him because he thought he could sell sand to the arabs!"

"Well, well, did he now?"

"Yes that's by all accounts. It's a very good opportunity at any rate. A very distinguished store."

Aunty Shirley was on the other side of me just a few yards behind as I sat in my sand fort still eating. On hearing their conversation she turned to a lady who wasn't an Aunty but who lived not far away from us in Hazelwood Close.

"Sacked again no doubt" she said in subdued tones, "Always got his hands in the till that Brian Reid" I swallowed hard and concentrated on my picnic.

 "He had to go to all the way to Charmsford to be able to get a new job. Go where his reputation hasn't gone before him so to speak. Why that poor woman puts up with him I'll never know." she continued.

"No! Poor Julie. Lovely girl, she came to my Tupperware Party only a few weeks ago. I thought then that she could do so much better." said the other lady.

"Frightened of him" said Shirley "He's free with his fists that one. Indoors at any rate. Not so brave down the pub against blokes but he'll give her a knock if she steps out of line."

As I sat there in the full midday sunshine I felt my head pulse and fill with heat. I tried but I couldn't stop it and my eyes filled. I licked a salty tear away from my cheek quickly with my tongue. I had lost all interest in my lunch now and could not eat. My skin prickled with the heat but I dared not move.

"Sees himself as a ladies' man too. Quite the womaniser. Went off on a dirty weekend with some slapper called Sandra from the biscuit factory only a few weeks ago. His mum and his sister think the sun shines out of his behind. They don't know the half of it. Poor Julie."

I had held back the rest of my tears but I felt sick. I scrunched up my crisp packet noisily to draw attention to myself but they didn't seem to register my presence and just carried on talking about Tupperware and Avon and which offered the best commission rates to housewives. I passed my rubbish over to Nanna who was showing a knitting pattern in her magazine to Aunty Cathy. Michael was on the other side of them now continuing to dig his expanding channel of water. Tammy and Dawn were back and were laid flat out behind Aunty Shirley snoozing on their floral towels and so I wandered back down to the shore to find a nice pebble to take home for Mummy. There were so many very pretty ones in the shallows but when I picked them up and the sun dried them in my hands they never looked quite so good as they had done down in the sandy shingle.

I decided instead to keep my 50p so I could give that to her as a present when we got home. I knew she never had very much money, perhaps it would help.

That night after Nanna and Aunty Cathy had gone home and I was back in my own bedroom I was woken up by the familiar sounds of arguing and furniture moving heavily downstairs. It had been a little while but I knew what to expect.

I was groggy with sleep and heat but I got out of bed quietly and waited on the top of the stairs for Michael to come out of his room for us to listen and wait together until it stopped. I put my arm around him and we cried silently until the final crash and a door slam. I could smell the salt of the sea still lingering in Michaels hair as I gave his shoulders a squeeze. Then when it went quiet again I took him back to bed. I kissed him goodnight, snuggled his teddy under his arm and walked backwards out of the room keeping an eye on him until his breathing became the regular breathing of sleep so I could silently close his bedroom door.

Back in my bed I strained my ears to listen for any other sounds or indications of danger. The night was still and I could hear Mummy sobbing downstairs. Daddy had gone out.

The telly was on very quietly in the living room. I took a few moments and tuned my ears into it's frequency so I could hear what she was watching.

Demis Roussous a huge Greek man in a kaftan began singing in a falsetto voice. He was number one in the hit parade and we had all laughed when he came onto Top of the Pops because he looked so unusual and funny. Daddy called him the 'bearded lady' but then he had a nickname for everyone, even himself.

What a sad sounding song. "Foreever and eever and eever and eever you'll be the one………" It sounded even sadder in the dark of the hot night, eerie even. I really didn't like it, it wasn't my kind of pop song but as I lay there I found myself listening to it quite intently, it was better than hearing my Mummy crying.

PART TWO
Don't Go Breaking My Heart

"Don't go breaking my heart

I couldn't if I tried

Aw honey if I get restless

Baby you're not that kind"

CHAPTER THIRTEEN

Daddy had suddenly decided we were going to have a party. Although we had lived in Sycamore Drive for well over a year, we had never really had a housewarming he said. We would show the locals what a good party looked like, he also said.

He had given Mummy some money to get herself something nice to wear from Chelsea Girl which was her favourite shop. All the Aunties and Uncles from the street were invited and some people from where Mummy and Daddy work but not Nanna. The only real Aunty, Aunty Cathy might also come with some friends from her factory where she made holes in sheets of metal day in day out. Michael and I were the only children invited and we could stay up for a little while, have some party food and then go to bed when Mummy said so.

We all had extra jobs to do to make the house look nice, mine was to sweep down the stairs and then hoover the hallway. Michael cleaned out Herbert and put his toys away so as usual he got off lightly. My mum was a good cook and she was making little open pies called vol au vents which we were excited about as we had never had these before. They had different fillings, but these didn't look all that nice to me though I could see Michael was interested. She was going to do some special ones with sandwich spread in for me and of course they would be sausages on sticks and my very favourite treat – cheese and pineapple on sticks. There would be peanuts and crisps too and Corona Dandelion & Burdock just for us. Mummy said we could stay up a little bit later than usual so we could say hello to everyone and have some treats before we went up to sleep out of the way of the grown ups.

Dad sorted his records out on the sideboard thingy which had a turntable inside. If you stacked a load of them up they would play one after another as one finished and the next was released and landed on top.

His friend Don came round early in the day with some booze – lots of brown bottles and something called a party 7 and Mummy had some Babycham for herself and her friends and people were to bring 'bottles'. Every surface was cleaned and every knick-knack positioned just so. There was a tense atmosphere and after lunch mum released us and said we could go out to play for a few hours whilst they got on with getting everything ready. After a while Daddy must have started to get on her nerves too because when we were in the wood park he walked through and said he was on the way to the pub to get out of her way for a bit.

Us kids had competitions to see who could swing the swing the highest and who could go up and down the slide the most times without stopping and the shade of the trees and the company of the gang was soothing. Dawn and Tammy and I practised some of the routines for the gang show and the boys played that tag where you are immune if you are off the ground.

Teatime approached so I was relieved Michael was in one piece as I told him we needed to get home. We hadn't seen Dad pass back through the park, perhaps he had gone home the long way round.

He wasn't there so we had our cheese on toast sat at the breakfast bar and then Mummy let us watch some telly whilst she went upstairs to have a bath. She put us in the tepid rose fragrant water after her and then in our nicest pyjamas. She brushed out our hair so we both looked nice. Then she took off her housecoat and put on her new dress. It was a maxi dress, black and emerald green with sliver glittery bits. She even wore some make up, some green colour around her dark green eyes lined dramatically with some black like Cleopatra.

"Mummy you look very pretty" said Michael and she really did. She had done something complicated with her hair too and it was backcombed and stylish and although we were all nearly choking from the liberal use of hairspray she looked like a film star and her dress sparkled.

The dining table was decked out with a crisp linen cloth and a hitherto unseen range of delights were presented upon it. There were candles on the mantle shelf and fresh ash trays positioned around the long living room. The evening was warm so the windows were ajar and the curtains partially opened. Mum had turned off the overhead lights and had lamps on in the corners of the room.

Aunty Shirley and Uncle Sandy were the first to arrive followed by Aunty Doreen and Uncle Roger from Larch Drive. Aunty Shirley was in the brightest flowing flouncy red creation that Little Loxwood or I at any rate, had ever seen and even Uncle Sandy looked a little overwhelmed by her ostentatious appearance. Her hair was also quite big and it made a flammable reddish halo around her heavily and professionally made up face. She had put her cigarette in a long cigarette holder for the occasion.

Then Aunty Beryl came with Uncle Tom and after them Uncle Ed and Aunty Janice from across the road. They were kind and friendly and were wowed by the vol au vents. They weren't quite as glamorously dressed as Aunty Shirley but everyone looked nice in summer dresses for the ladies and short sleeved shirts for the men. Next to arrive were Don and Craig who were from Dad's old work, they were in their plastic looking suits as usual and then people appeared whose connexions to us or whose names I wasn't all that sure of.

Aunty Cathy arrived with a chap she introduced to us as, her friend Trevor. She had on a turquoise dress suit that Nanna had made and it complimented her hair and she looked stunning. There were quite a lot of people squeezing into our small house.

As Mummy made people welcome it became more and more obvious that there was something not quite right and one essential ingredient was missing, the host – our Daddy. I had almost forgotten about him and the fact that this whole thing was his big idea in the first place. We were all so busy greeting people, offering food and smiling shyly he had totally slipped off our radar. The house looked nice and there was a pleasant atmosphere. Uncle Ed had sorted out the records on the record player and people were smoking, drinking, chatting and starting to tentatively sway to the background music.

I noticed Mummy had a very sophisticated glass in her hand. It had a tiny picture of Bambi with a large blue bowed ribbon around his neck embossed on the side. I instantly loved that fragile looking glass that must have previously lived somewhere out of reach as I had never seen it before. She had a cigarette in her other hand and was chatting to the man from the chip shop where she worked. She was smiling and laughing and she looked radiant.

"Spangle, Michael come here a moment and say hello to Uncle Kevin." Although we had seen him down the parade and had been in the chip shop many times we still both felt shy. We stood there in our nightclothes with blank tired little faces.

"Perhaps it's time I took you two up to bed." Mum said.

"I'm not even tired." lied Michael stifling a yawn.

"Five more minutes then I'll take you up. I'll just finish my cigarette first." Uncle Kevin smiled at us both in what he probably thought was a friendly way. He was quite fat and had greasy looking hair. He was very smartly dressed though in a suit and on such a hot evening.

"This is one of my favourite songs, Julie." he said as Rod Stewart started singing 'Tonight's the Night'.

"Mine too. I love Rod Stewart." Mummy responded happily. She did as well, she was always playing his albums. They started singing along with the words together and then Mum laughed coyly and said, "I think I had better get these two up into bed. Say goodnight to Uncle Kevin kids." We both dutifully did. He half smiled awkwardly and Mummy took us to say goodnight to some of the other Aunties and Uncles.

"Brian's running a bit late I see." Said Aunty Shirley as Mummy led us upstairs.

 "I'm sure he won't be long." Mummy replied and took us up to do our teeth and tucked us into our beds.

As I lay between my nylon sheets, too hot for blankets, I could hear the soft murmur of music and chatter. There were occasional ripples of laughter and before long I felt myself drifting off to sleep on a cushion of warm night air.

It probably wasn't all that much later that I awoke startled as the front door slammed and the frame shuddered slightly. I heard raised voices and crashing and the music momentarily was turned up louder and then back down again. There was laughter and a bang and then the party continued at a higher volume than before. It seemed Daddy had come back from the pub and had bought all the clientele along with him. My body felt tense as the newly charged atmosphere from downstairs permeated its way up to me in my bed in my little bedroom above.

I could hear people chatting in the garden as the house became unable to contain everyone and people were drawn out into the summer air. The music got a little raunchier and I think I could hear Daddy singing loudly along. There was more laughter and then I could hear Daddy's voice raised talking loudly to someone, though I could not tell what he was saying as there were so many competing noises.

Then I heard the sitting room door open and I could hear someone charging up the stairs. Daddy had gone into Michaels room. I got up and went into the hallway as he came out, "Spangle, Spangle come downstairs. Let me show everyone my beautiful kids." He slurred. He had Michael by the arm and was pulling him along. "There's someone here I

80

want you both to meet." Michael looked bemused and more than half asleep. As we all entered the living room even the muted lighting seemed very bright and exposing and it was hard not to feel alarmed by the sight of so many people, many of whom were strangers. "Turn off the music a moment Don, turn it off! Attention everyone, attention please. I just want to introduce you all to my wonderful children! A pair of little angles aren't they?" It took a while for the room to fully quieten down. People turned to look at us properly and there was an expectant lull in the room as people weren't sure how to react to the situation. Daddy pushed us both forward so that we were standing in front of him.

I felt uncomfortable and tired and still no one in the room spoke and then Daddy said

"These two kids are probably the only good things I have ever done in my life." His voice was small and then Mummy said, "For God's sake Brian!" she looked shocked and took a step forwards towards us. Then

"Shut up, you bloody miserable cow, shut bloody up" The room was silent. I could see Aunty Shirley's strangulated expression. Dad was pulling us along over to the sideboard and he started talking to us directly now, a little bit more gently.

"There's someone special to me who I want you both to meet." He tugged us over to his friend Don. Don looked as gormless as ever with his fluffy hair and big sideburns. Stood next to Don, slightly behind him was an oldish woman. She was dressed in a tailored dark purple trousers suit with a pink satiny blouse underneath. She had a lot of collars and her neckline was busy and distracting. This lady wore a lot of jewellery and had more gold rings on her fingers than I had ever seen before. She had a short bobbed hairstyle and looked very grown up, much older than Mum and Dad. But not as old as Nanna.

"Spangle, Michael" Daddy said " this is your Aunty Rita." Me and Michael looked at each other then at her. Dad pushed us both towards her. We said nothing.

"Hello" she said smiling at us. "It's nice to meet you both, I have heard so much about you from your father Samantha. And you too of course Michael. You are right Brian they are both very beautiful children." She bent down and leaned forward to look at us as though we were specimens in a jar. Perhaps she needed glasses and she couldn't see us properly without getting uncomfortably close.   A stomach-churning silence filled the room. Then,

"Have you got children Rita?" it was Aunty Shirley.

Rita looked a little startled and stood up straight again "Yes, a boy and a girl too."

"A lot older I expect?"

"Yes" said Rita, her previously confident manner draining a bit.

"So you're married?" Aunty Shirley was raising herself up to her full, rather imposing height.

"Er yes."

"Separated" said my Daddy somewhat sharply.

"Any grandchildren yet?" someone laughed and Aunty Shirley turned her back on Aunty Rita in a very dismissive way before she even had time to answer.

People started talking to each other again and Mum came over. She gave Daddy a hard look and took a hand of each of ours. She turned and led me and Michael through the sea of guests towards the door. Daddy seemed to suddenly sober up and looked momentarily abashed. Aunty Rita looked awkward but then said loudly,

"Well goodnight then children. It was very nice to meet you. See you both again soon." My Mum made a snorting sound and dragged us upstairs. She tucked us in hastily holding back tears. She kissed me on the forehead.

"Love you Mummy" I said trying not to cry because I knew instinctively that would start her off. "Love you Spangle." Although I had no idea what had just happened I knew it wasn't good and as soon as she had closed the door I started sobbing into the pillow till it was all wet.

Not long after she had gone back down I could hear the front door opening and people saying goodbye and thank you for inviting us as they slowly filed out and left. The music was still on and I could hear the sounds of clearing up and the washing up bowl below me being filled up. I could hear talking but had no idea how many people or who was still there. I was no longer tired just hyper alert and I registered movement from Michaels bedroom too.

I padded across the landing to check up on him.

He was standing on his Lego box looking out of his window. I could see that the sky was clear and studded with twinkling stars. The moon was full and yellow hanging grotesquely above the tallest trees that we could just see the tops of from the wood park behind the houses opposite. I climbed up next to him and looked down at the street. It was very well lit and we could see Uncle Ed and Uncle Sandy standing outside Uncle Ed's house across the road. They were talking but too quietly for us to hear. We could see a few other people drifting off in different directions too but it looked like Sandy and Ed might be watching our house.

Suddenly there was a massive smash from downstairs. Mummy was screaming and I could hear Don saying,

"Cool it Brian, cool it mate." Me and Michael crept to the hallway and took up our seat on the top of the stairs.

"I never liked that ugly ash tray anyway." Dad snorted. "Nag nag bloody nag, I've had a bloody nuff." Dad was shouting.

"Can't you see what I have to put up with Don? A bloody nuff!" I heard Aunty Rita interjecting,

"Come on Brian, you're just tired I really think we ought to just help Julie clear up this mess and then I'll go."

"No, go now! Just go, get out, both of you. GO!" shouted Mum. At that moment Uncle Ed and Uncle Sandy came back in the front door and marched past us children invisible on the top of the stairs. Uncle Ed coughed loudly on entering the living room and said assertively

"Right Brian, I think Julie's right, it would make sense if you went and stayed somewhere else tonight. Sleep it off."

There were a few moments of silence and then some movement. Dad must have felt out numbered because he came out to the hallway to take his suede jacket off the peg. He looked up and saw us both, as he did so he waved a shaky arm up to us.

"Alright kids, off to bed with you!" he smiled nicely. "Great party until your bloody mother went and spoilt it all." He cocked his head and gave us his wink. Uncle Sandy came through the door and looked at us both sitting huddled on the top stair.

"Come on Brian! It's time you left" Uncle Sandy said and then Aunty Rita emerged.

"Let's walk down to the phone box and call a taxi Brian. It's alright we'll go and get out of the way. He can come with me. I'll take care of him." She said this last bit in a pointed way, looking directly at Uncle Sandy. Daddy looked a bit sheepish then. He was clearly very drunk and could hardly hold his body up straight let alone walk. Somehow she firmly manoeuvred him to the front door and outside. Mummy came into the hallway and rushed up the stairs to us in floods of tears.

"Sorry kids, sorry" she kept saying between sobs and she took us both into Michaels room. We all three sat on Michaels bed crying for a few minutes and then Mummy put him gently under the covers and put his teddy under his arm as usual. As we walked back across the landing to my room Don stuck his head through the living room door.

"Don't worry Julie, love, we'll clear up. It'll all be alright." Mum ignored him and took me to my room. She put me into bed and then laid down bedside me. She had smudgy black make up rings all around her eyes and dark rivulets were etched down her cheeks. I put my arm around her and we stopped crying and listened to the men tiding up down stairs. After a little while we fell asleep like that.

CHAPTER FOURTEEN

When I woke up the next morning I had no idea of what time it might be. It was sunny but then it always was lately. I could hear Mummy moving around downstairs as usual. The kettle was whistling on the stove and I could hear her setting the breakfast things out. The radio was on but at a quiet level. The recollection of the events of the previous night slowly seeped back into my consciousness and for a few moments I felt overwhelmed. My head felt heavy and I felt a little sick. Then I pulled myself together and blew my nose. I got out of my bed and drew open my curtains fully. Birds were singing, it was another glorious day.

I went to look for Michael. I looked in through his bedroom door and could see he wasn't there. The bathroom door was ajar and I could see he wasn't in there and there were no sounds from the toilet. He must have got up already. I went down stairs quietly and poked my head in the front room. Curtains open. The room looked neat and tidy with no incriminating evidence of the scene from last night anywhere. Empty apart from the lingering aroma of stale cigarette ash.

I could see Mummy was in the kitchen dressed in jeans and a nice gypsy looking top. She looked tired and tear stained but quite normal really. I went into the kitchen and she came over and kissed me on the top of my head, "Boiled egg and soliders?" she smiled. I nodded, I still couldn't see Michael, he wasn't sat at the breakfast bar in his usual place. "Run up and fetch Michael, will you Spangle?" Mum said.

He must have been in the toilet so I went up to find him. Not in the toilet, not in the bathroom. Crikey, what next with that boy? My alarm bells were all ringing but I was getting more than a bit fed up with Michael's antics, had he gone out to play, had he run away? Nothing would surprise me. Or so I thought because as I stood helpless in the middle of his room I could hear soft weeping. It sounded some distance away and I felt confused. I listened carefully, it was crying and it was Michael crying.

"Michael, Michael" I called softly, "Where are you?" I looked under his bed and in his wardrobe, nothing. The crying seemed to have stopped.

"Michael, I've had enough of this. What are you playing at, where are you?" I hissed.

"I'm here Spangle."

"Where?" and then it dawned on me that his voice was coming from outside. I went over to the window and stood on the Lego box. His window was wide open and I could see little signs of life at this end of the street. A cat slinked around the corner garage opposite but that was about it. The garden looked empty. I peered around again.

"Spangle!" He sounded close by. O my God, he was close by, I looked down and about four feet below the window ledge, in his pyjamas on the milky glass porch roof sat Michael. He was crouched as closely to the house wall as possible almost clinging onto it for dear life. He had no slippers on his little feet. A paper plate of vol au vents and other remnants of food was placed next to him and he was sobbing and dishevelled.

"Gosh Michael, what on earth are you doing?"

"Help me Spangle, I'm stuck."

"Well I can see that. What are you doing out there? How did you get down there?"

"I didn't mean to."

"That's what you always say. 'I didn't mean to.' I have had it up to here with you!" I said realising as I said it that I sounded exactly like Mummy. He started to cry.

"But I didn't mean it. I was scared. I've been out here all night. I'm cold Spangle. I didn't mean it" I pushed the window open as widely as it would go and tried to lean over to reach him. I couldn't I was just too little.

"I tried to climb back in but all those bits of small stones stuck on the wall scratched my hands and there was nothing to hold onto." Michael snivelled. He showed me his hands and they were grazed and bloodied. Stupid, ugly pebbledash. I was feeling cross now none of this made any sense.

"What are you doing with that plate of food? Where did it come from?"

"I went downstairs in the night. I felt hungry and I just took it from the kitchen. There was so much food left so I bought some up to my room for a midnight feast." I couldn't help smiling. I had told him about midnight feasts which I had discovered from reading my boarding school books.

"I still don't understand why you are out there. That's not a proper place to have a midnight feast. You are so naughty Michael!"

"I was going to eat it in bed then I got worried about the crumbs so I thought I should eat it at the windowsill so I could sweep any crumbs outside." Good thinking, I thought.

"But then I saw Dad coming back and didn't want him to see I had taken them. He would have hit me if he found food in my room so I threw it all out the window. There were lots of glasses and plates out there so no one would have known it was me." This boy was not as green as he was cabbage looking, I thought

"But it all landed on the porch" he started whimpering again. "Daddy will go mad if he finds out. I had to climb down to try and get rid of it all but then I couldn't get back up"

This was beyond belief. He was sobbing now.

"I tried and tried. I didn't mean it."

"You've been there all night? If Daddy catches you he will kill you for definite" I felt desperately sorry for him.

"Get me in Spangle, please, I promise I will never do anything naughty again!" I laughed at that and even he smiled. I had a bright idea. "Stay there." I said rather unnecessarily.

I crept downstairs nimbly but I knew Mum must be wondering why I was taking so long. I still had my nighty on, but I turned left at the bottom of the stairs towards the front door instead of right into the living room. I opened it as quietly as I could and popped it on the latch. Then I slipped outside and climbed up onto the metal frame. I got quite a long way up in the ironwork but I could only just reach the roof and was not able to clamber onto it or reach to anywhere near Michael.

"Michael, why don't you come over here to the edge and I can help you climb down?"

"I can't move. I tried that, it's too slippy." I could see the glass was convex and what a bad position he was in. He could easily slip off and it was high for such a little boy. He looked terrified. Suddenly he kicked the plate of tired looking party food towards me with his foot.

"Get rid of it, please Spangle. Don't let Dad see." I pulled the plate towards me and as it reached the edge the vol au vents all fell on the grass.

"I don't think he's here. But we need to get you down before he docs come back. He's not going to like this."

"He did come back, I saw him. He came back in his car. That's why I had to climb out here to get the little pies back." I think Michael was over tired and must have been hallucinating last night.

"Daddy hasn't got a car, you know that."

"Yes he has, that green one"

"Michael, you've lost your mind. How the heck am I going to get you down? I am going to have to get Mum. We need a ladder or something." He started crying wildly.

"Stay still. It will be alright." I was quickly and silently saying my prayer in my head. Please god, make everything turn out right. What if Dad was really back and in the house? He might hear us and come and see what was going on. He would go mad. Should I tell Mummy? She might get upset again. I hate seeing her cry. I climbed down and stood on the path looking up at Michaels' little body through the glass. A red and blue shape of brushed cotton pyjamas.

Miraculously (had God just answered my prayer?) Uncle Ed opened his front door to get his milk in and he looked across and saw me. He was still in his pyjamas too. He looked puzzled and then he smiled as he walked across the road towards us.

"Well, well, well." he said. His tone was kind. "What a funny turn of events." He nimbly climbed onto the metal frame and stood himself up on one of its joists making his head stick over the top of the porch roof so he could look directly at Michael. He smiled and calmly instructed him.

"Now son. I want you to lie down slowly onto your tummy. There's a good boy. Facing towards me. Slowly. Put your arms out in front of you. Well done now move along like a snake slowly towards me reaching out your hands. Go on, good boy." The blue and red shape inched closer to the edge where Uncle Ed was.

"Now don't be frightened, a little bit further until you can take my hand. That's it, good boy, keep moving slowly. Keep looking at me. Well done" A few minutes later Uncle Ed had a hold of him and had got him safely down onto the ground. He ruffled his hair and shooed us both back in the front door. He looked so gentlemanly in his stripy pyjamas and leather slippers. Why couldn't Uncle Ed be our father instead?

"Thank you Uncle Ed." I said

We both snuck back in and I unlatched the door. Then I remembered the vol au vents and paper plate and I dashed back out to get them. I flushed the vol au vents down the toilet after tearing them into little bits and I hid the paper plate in the laundry basket to throw away later. "Blimming heck" I thought, "That was close."

CHAPTER FIFTEEN

Michael was very well behaved for the rest of that day but that was probably just because he was exhausted after spending all night out on the porch roof. Daddy was back, Michael was right about that bit. I heard him snoring and slobbering in his bed as I went past their bedroom door to my own room to get dressed. The rancid smell of stale alcohol permeated, and I rushed to get away from it downstairs to Mummy. Michael was already at the counter eating Weetabix and Mummy looked up at me and smiled, "Did you fall back to sleep love? I suppose it was a very late night."

She set some colouring out on the big table for us to have something quiet to do, probably so there was less chance of us waking up Daddy. It was a very hot day and all the windows were open. A wasp buzzed lazily in and Mum had a Neil Diamond record on quietly. Sweet Caroline dum dum dum.... She was knitting on the sofa watching Michael and me. She was following what looked like a very complicated pattern. The day felt sultry yet calm.

"It's getting very hot." Mum said putting the needles and yarn down into her lap "Would you like me to put up the paddling pool?"

"I don't feel like it and anyway it takes ages to fill up." I said. I felt hot, tired and a bit grumpy.

"I'll do it Julie love. Would you like that kids?" We hadn't heard Daddy come into the room and all turned our heads toward the door as he awkwardly meandered in in his stale smelling dressing gown. He was smoking a cigarette and looked rough by anyone's measure.

"Yes please Dad" said Michael. "I would like to go in the pool." his face lit up as Daddy ruffled his hair. Mummy and I tensed recognising the inevitable fiasco that was likely to take up the rest of the afternoon as Dad faffed about trying to do something nice for everyone whether everyone liked it or not. We had some lunch and eventually he managed to set the pool up in under two hours just as the sun was starting to dip down a bit in the sky but it was still pleasant and a couple of kids from the gang started to emerge from wherever they had been all day and came to join us in the garden.

Mummy put biscuits and some left over party food out on trays and we were splashing happily about as dusk began to fall. It was unbelievably warm. Daddy and Mummy sat on deck chairs watching us with Dad falling in and out of sleep. Aunty Janice waved over at Mummy from across the road as she and Uncle Ed pulled up in their car with their kids Gary and Alison. Alison was older than us so we didn't really play with her. From the towels and lilos it looked as though they had just come back from a family day out at the beach. Uncle Ed put his hand on Aunty Janice's back as she bent to take something out of the boot. He seemed so gentle and so caring. Daddy was asleep and grunting in his deckchair. He was a bit purple and puffy and had stubble on his face. He looked like an angry troll. Uncle Ed looked so handsome.

Michael and Robert were doing handstands in the water and counting to see who could stay up the longest. Michael won and glowed when he received a word of praise from Daddy as he stirred from his slumber at just the right moment.

Mummy got up then and said, "I'll go in and make a start on the tea. Another half an hour kids then it'll be time to come in and get your night clothes on." Daddy made a noise of agreement and started to tidy up the towels and toys.

After a while Michael and Robert's splashing was starting to get on my nerves. Stacey and Dawn were getting cold too and us girls all started to get ready to go in.

"Are you coming in now Michael?" I asked

"Five more minutes" he said as he came up for air in the three inches of water that were left in the plastic pool. I went upstairs and put my nightie on and put my wet costume in the basket. I dried my hair in the towel and my skin felt taut and I realised the pool had been a good idea. I felt both refreshed and tired at the same time. I could hear Mummy in the kitchen below so thought it best to go and get Michael ready for tea.

He looked like he was getting cold and now Daddy had gone in and he had no audience it was easy to get him inside. As we came into the hall I could hear Mum and Dad talking,

"Hair of the dog, that's all Julie."

"It's a Sunday Brian, early closing is there any point in going out now?"

"It's back to work tomorrow Julie, a man needs to relax, go down the pub, see some faces. Anyway I really could do with a pint after the …"

"There's plenty here you can drink if that's all you need" Mummy's voice was getting higher, "but it's not JUST the booze is it Brian? Are you off to meet her, Rita, your fancy woman?"

"I've told you. We are just friends. She's like a mother figure to me. Couldn't cope at work without the support I get from Rita and if I lose this job……."

Silence from Mum, a sigh.

"Look Julie, I've been playing happy bloody families all bloody day. I don't know what more you want from me. I am getting dressed and going down the pub. End of."

"Don't you go breaking my heart Brian!" she said very softly.

"I won't Juliette. Of course I won't."

He came out into the hallway as we were making our way hurriedly upstairs. Mummy had followed him out but seeing us she held her tongue and went back into the lounge.

"Chip chop kids, get out of the way. Dad needs the bathroom first." He brusquely pushed us aside. As I got Michael into his bed clothes the smell of Old Spice started to pervade and even before we were downstairs for tea he was saying,

"Right kids, be good for your Mum. You'll see Dad the Bad in the morning."

CHAPTER SIXTEEN

The next morning Mummy was up early and she had me and Michael fed and dressed and ready to walk up Larch Road to the bus stop. We waited with two other ladies in the shelter trying to find a bit of shade. Thankfully we only waited a few minutes to catch the first of two buses to get us to Nanna's bungalow. Mummy said that we couldn't stay long as she had to get back in time for work at the chip shop at lunchtime as she chivvied us along. We changed buses at the bus station in Loxwood town centre and the second bus took a bit longer as it rattled along some country roads to the little town where Nanna lived.

The prefab looked a bit drab in the very bright sunshine. Bits of the pink paint were peeling off in places but it was nice to be coming to see Nanna. The bungalow was neat but it had a weary feel to it. It had been there longer than intended. The tiny hall and the front room were dark as Nanna let us in her front door. She was surprised and pleased to see us.

"Come in, come in" she said leading us through to the lighter and more roomy kitchen was which was the width of the back of the house. Today sunshine was pouring in through its sprucely clean net curtains, splashing across the surfaces of the room. The green of the trees and shrubs from the well-tended back garden cast a verdant hue on her tired and old-fashioned furnishings. Nanna gave me and Michael some orange squash in plastic beakers then she and Mum went into the other room together and once we had gulped down our drinks we followed.

In the dark living room there was a lot of very sturdy ancient furniture and a fancy mirror over a small coal fireplace. Even though it was the height of summer the coal scuttle was full and the grate was laid ready for any sudden plummeting of the thermometer.

There were several old sepia photos in frames on the inherited welsh dresser including a touching wedding photo of Nanna and Grandad Harold. Nanna had told us about this picture many times. It was her pride and joy and was taken as a favour by a photographer that she used to clean for. He had given it to them as a wedding present. Outside the old Chapel porch Grandad Harold stood very rigidly looking at the camera in earnest. He was in his army uniform which bore a single medal and she wore a delicate floral dress she had hand sewn herself. Nanna had fresh flowers in a headdress in her hair, she looked terribly young but happy in a serious way.

Their happiness had been brief as he had died only a few years after returning from the war, leaving Nanna to bring up their children alone. She was too proud to ever even consider remarrying and anyway what happened to her beloved Harold had been God's will. Despite being badly injured and having shrapnel in his leg it was a bus that had killed him when he was crossing a road on his way to visit his own mother. His mobility had been affected by his injury in a bomb blast and he had had a bad limp so he hadn't been able to get out of the way.

There was a rather sweet old photo of Daddy and Aunty Cathy as children stood in their Sunday best at the front gate. The clothes were so old fashioned, Daddy in a little suit and tie. The tie matching the ribbon in his little sisters' hair. They must have been younger than Michael and I when it was taken. Daddy smiled broadly, cheekily, whilst a younger Aunty Cathy stared at her shoes.

Nanna sat down beside the dresser in her straight backed winged armchair. This was gold and green and had little bits of embroidered cloth on each arm rest and there was a matching one where her head rested on the back. She had stitched these herself along with the many other embroidered items that decorated all the rooms in the bungalow. The little prefab was her domain and a shrine to the few happy years she had enjoyed with brave Harold. They had laid out the garden together and furnished the rooms and that's how she wanted her home to stay. She had never got over him and looked forward to the day when she would eventually die and be reunited with him in heaven. Was Grandad Harold an angel, I wondered, was he looking down on us right now as Nanna believed?

"There's jam tarts in the tin on the kitchen table." Nanna said to us and Michael was out the door before she had finished the sentence. I don't like jam but I followed Michael to make sure he didn't get up to anything. Nanna's old ginger cat was curled up on a cushion in the sunshine by the back door. Michael lay down next to him smoothing him with one hand whilst eating jam tart with the other. I loitered close to the living room door with Michael squarely in my line of vision.

"I don't know what to do or what to think. I really don't. He says it's just a friendship and he won't turn his back on her and I have to accept it. He says she's like a mother to him." I heard Mummy confide to Nanna

"Hmmp a mother figure indeed. What is that supposed to mean, he's got a perfectly good mother, is he saying I'm not a good mother after all the sacrifices I've made bringing him and Cathy up alone? Scrimping and struggling after my Harold died?"

"I don't have a clue what he means Gwen. Except she's a bit older than him so perhaps he means that." Mum sounded sad. "He swears there's nothing in it. Plutonic, just friends, he says. Didn't look like that. The way they looked at each other. Didn't look or feel that way. He's breaking my heart Gwen"

"Well if he says there's nothing in it Julie then there's nothing in it. He's not leaving you or asking you for a divorce is he? "

"How can I trust him Gwen, it's not as if it would be the first time?"

"But he always comes back to you and the kids doesn't he? His family."

"I don't know if I can just keep on putting up with it. I deserve better."

"Deserve better? Who's been filling your head up with these things? He's your husband Julie. God put you together. You made vows!"

"So did Brian but those vows don't seem to mean anything to him. I don't seem to mean anything to him. God knows Gwen. Even the kids don't. Not really. When he's had a drink, well….. well when he's sober too to be honest, he cares about no one but himself" Mummy was crying as she spoke now.

"It's a man's world. I did my best with him. But there was no father to keep him in check. Perhaps I should have been firmer with him but I spared the rod. A woman alone, Brian was the man of the house after he had gone. My Harold must be turning in his grave. The good Lord tests us all Julie. Julie, don't cry dear"

I came back into the room and Mum sniffed back her tears and dried her eyes, she turned to me

"Alright love? Where's Michael?"

"He's gone in the garden with Marmalade"

"Put the kettle on Spangle." said Nanna "There's just time for a quick cup of tea before you catch the bus back"

I went back to the kitchen and set about making them tea. The kettle boiled and I warmed the pot. Through the window I could see Michael digging a hole in a vegetable border with an old spoon. One of his favourite pass times. He had his shorts on and a stripey tee shirt and he looked like butter wouldn't melt. His hair was white and tousled with the effects of this summer. He seriously looked like an angel.

"Brian always was wilful as a child. And selfish too if I am honest. Harold spoiled him when he was a little boy. Adored him." I could hear Nanna saying. "He wasn't a good brother. bullied Cathy. I know he can be nasty like that."

"I do love him Gwen but he's no good."

"He'll settle as he gets older, calm down a bit….. Perhaps."

"I don't know what to do for the best."
"What do you mean, do? Decent women don't get divorced Julie if that's what you are thinking. You are married in the sight of God."

"The situation, it's not good for the kids. The arguing, well it's just spiteful Gwen. He will hurt me in any way he can. I try to be a good wife……O Spangle, thank you love. Just what Mummy needed, a nice cup of tea."

"Thank you Spangle." said Nanna as I put her cup and saucer down at her side.

"Would you take the bowl and pick me a few peas for my tea later on and pick a few extra for you to take home. If you and Michael go down to the patch at the bottom you may find a few tasty raspberries still on the canes as well."

I sighed loudly but went out with the plastic bowl and did as I was asked. By the time I came back in they were in the kitchen and Mummy was rinsing the cups. Nanna gave me a smile when I gave her the bowl of peas.

"Pass me my handbag. I am sure I've got a 10p each in there for you and Michael to get some sweeties on the way home."

Michael wandered in with mud around his mouth and we all started laughing as Nanna said, "Though Michael won't want any as he'll be full up with all that mud that he loves so much."

We got home in time for Mummy to go to work and Michael and I stayed in and played Lego until she got back. She seemed happier than she had done earlier and she had bought us home some chips and sausages. I tidied away all the Lego and then we were allowed to go out and play with the gang before bed. Mummy was humming a Rod Stewart song to herself as she hoovered around as me and Michael made our exit.

CHAPTER SIXTEEN

It was a glorious warm evening, the sun streaked sky, gold, orange and pink. The melody of the ice cream van floated by and it seemed like every kid in the neighbourhood was out. There were so many colourful variations of shorts and tee shirts, summer dresses and sandals on display that evening on the streets of Little Loxwood. All the kids were browner than they had ever been in their short lives and there was a whiff of olive oil and vinegar in the air as Seventies mothers believed this to be the very best combo to put on summer skin. A few were peeling and several of us had freckles hitherto unseen.

I told Michael firmly that I would not take any nonsense this evening and that he had better not injure himself in any way, shape or form. I used my strictest voice. He looked very shame faced but did not reply so I laid down the law and told him I would mention the vol au vents incident to Daddy if he did anything naughty or dangerous. His face blanched so I felt sure he had got the message.

Philip and Gary deftly organised a huge game of bulldog on the far end green. There must have been about fifteen kids out on that small patch of grass and those two boys were born leaders. They had us in teams in no time with no real moaning and with everyone working together and getting along. It was noisy, it was fun and it was exhausting. Bursts of loud cheering and silvery tinkles of childish laughter hung in the evening air.

When we had chased and caught each other just enough for one evening some of us stayed on the green in smaller groups chatting and playing - sweaty and laughing. All the kids were good natured and enjoying the freedom the heatwave was affording us. Phillip's dad Uncle Des had tied some thick rope and a piece of wood from a high branch of the tree that stood in the green's centre and we took turns to swing on it and spin each other around. Some of the kids from further away streets started to wander off home and the dusk was turning darker. Michael was behaving and he was playing marbles on the adjacent pavement with Robert.

Most of the girls my age had gone in but Dawn and I practised some of the songs from the gang show. We knew all the words already we just needed to get the timing of the actions a little tighter. We lay ourselves down on the dry grass. We chatted about the gang show and the other Brownies. I looked at the light navy sky. It was streaked with dark pink and was very beautiful. I was starting to feel tired. The street was now quieter. It had been a long day. Without seeing her face I could almost hear Dawn thinking next to me. She swallowed then from nowhere -

"Are your parents getting a divorce?" Dawn suddenly blurted out. I was shocked. I could somehow tell she was too. I felt her embarrassment. I didn't really know what to say. I looked straight ahead at the beautiful darkening sky. I had never thought about that word before and now I had heard it twice in one day. It was unusual to even say it.

"No. No. I don't know. Why did you ask that?" She was silent for a moment as she considered her answer. I still didn't turn to look at her but I could feel her looking at me.

"My Mum says divorce is getting more common nowadays." "Is it? Is she getting divorced?" I asked.

"I don't think so, though she does say that my dad is a moronic idiot and she wishes she had never set eyes on him." We both burst out laughing. I looked at her squarely.

"I'm never getting married." I said, "Me neither" said Dawn.

I wandered across the green to get Michael and as I did something compelled me to look up the hill towards the main road. There was a dark Morris car parked a short way up and the inside light was on as two people sat inside. Had I seen that car before? I realised it was Daddy and Aunty Rita and Daddy was in the driver's seat. They were talking intently, heads close together.

Suddenly, in an instant they were kissing. Amorously.

I looked away, shocked heat seared through me. I heard Michael call me and I dashed over to him turning my back to the scene I had witnessed, blocking it from his innocent gaze. We put his marbles in his cloth bag and I dragged him quickly home.

When we got in Mummy was tidying up and making Daddy's tea. We got ready for bed as usual and came downstairs ready to watch a programme on telly before bed. Mummy gave us a slice of bread and marmite each which was totally delicious.

Daddy strolled in from work at his usual time in his smart clothes. Was that a newer, nicer suit? He looked especially smug. He had had a haircut and he smelt even more groomed than usual.

He took his jacket off and put his slippers on as he settled himself noisily in his special chair pointed at the telly. Mummy was putting cheese, pickles and crackers on a plate for him, whilst his food finished cooking. He had a carrier bag with the name of the shop he worked in, Hartley's, on the floor next to his feet.

"Come here kids" he said to us in a conspiratorial way. Before I could ask why Michael was in his lap and so I got down from the settee and went over to his chair. "Pass me the shopping bag up Spangle." He said with a wink, "Anyone around here like presents?"

"Me, me!" said little Michael, traitor!

"Good!" said Dad, "Let's see what we have here then. Umm a Matchbox police car and ambulance set who could that be for?" Michael more or less snatched it from his hand "and a Mallory Towers box set?" my mouth dropped, a complete set of my favourite books. I already had some of these, what an extravagant present. I felt Mummy appear behind me,

"O how thoughtful Brian. Children say thank you to your father, gosh your very favourite things."

"And there's something else in here too." Dad continued. He looked up at her bashfully and pulled out a bottle of Mum's signature cologne Charlie Girl. I masked a wince as Mummy flushed with happiness as he handed it to her.

"That's for you my Juliette. From your Romeo" She flushed, looked at us and then lent in to kiss him.

"Thanks love." Mummy said visibly flustered. She went back out to the kitchen where something was boiling and Daddy pulled me up onto his lap too.

"And one more thing each." He said his hand back in the bag, "and this is from your Aunty Rita. A walnut whip each!" We never had chocolate except at Christmas so this would have been surprising on its own. The fact that it was from Aunty Rita made it unsettling. I observed a frown on Michaels brow but he took it anyway and we went back to the settee and ate them before bed. Dad happily argued with someone on Nationwide whilst Mummy served up his dinner on a tray for him. He kicked off his slippers and put his feet up on his pouffe. I heard him mutter, oblivious to everyone but me, maybe oblivious even to himself, "King of the Castle."

After Mummy had tucked us in she said that I was allowed to have ten minutes to read. My mind was too busy digesting recent events and I could not concentrate on reading. Of course I loved the books and of course I would read them but my mind was all over the place. I turned off my lamp and opened the curtains a little to see the stars. There was a hint of a breeze and the air was getting cooler and it felt nice to be snuggled up in my bed so I decided to be bold when saying my prayers tonight. I did my usual and asked God to look after everybody by name but then I changed a bit and at the end asked – Dear God, thank you for everything, please make everything turn out right and ....please God please make Daddy run off with Aunty Rita and leave us alone and never come back. Thank you, God. Forever and ever. Amen.

CHAPTER SEVENTEEN

Mummy wanted to take me and Michael shopping for new school clothes with her chip shop money. She asked us to come down the parade after she had finished work to meet her and then we would catch a bus to Charmsford where Daddy's shop was. She thought it would make a change from Loxwood and that it would be nice to go in and surprise him and say hello whilst he was at work. Michael seemed very keen but it didn't feel like such a good idea to me.

It took quite a while to get to the austere old-fashioned town of Charmsford. Michael pressed his pale little face against the window and stared out silently at the world passing by. He always got the window seat when we went on the bus, it wasn't fair. The bus seemed to make a million stops before pulling up at the dusty old bus station.

Mum took us to a children's clothing shop first and didn't find anything she liked so then we went to Clarkes and had our feet measured for school shoes. She bought a nice sensible black pair for Michael and said she would get me my new school shoes when she next got paid. I didn't mind, going back to school seemed impossible to imagine with the sun still blasting down on us on a daily basis. I was getting shopping fatigue and Michael was clearly flagging too so Mum herded us towards the façade of Hartleys, the shop where Daddy was currently flaunting his sales skills. It was quite different from the other shops Mummy usually took us to and had a faded grandeur. It looked as if it had been there from the days when everything was still in black and white even though it was crazily colourful inside.

The stately main entrance was a carpeted lobby. It boasted two ornate metal lifts either side of a wide sweeping staircase. A large gilded wooden board proudly positioned to the right of it told you what was sold on the different floors. Mummy inspected this carefully and then asked us if we would like to go up in a lift. We most certainly would! There was even an actual attendant inside it and it had a folding metal gate. It felt very stylish to travel up to the third floor in this with a uniformed man pressing the desired buttons for us. Me and Michael looked at each other and had a silent snigger. I looked at Mummy and she did look a little less confident now that we were nearing her chosen destination. I almost felt I should stop it all or say something at the very least but then the doors slowly parted and opened out onto a brightly, artificially lit shop floor.

We all stepped out a little gingerly and as the lift pinged shut again it suddenly dawned on me that the whole place was a bit like that program on the telly called 'Are you being Served?" Mummy looked around gaining her bearings. A very young man in an overtight suit appeared before us as if from nowhere and asked if he could help us. We were all a little taken aback at being spoken to.

"Er…Yes Please. Is Mr Reid available?" Mum said politely.

"Of course, madam. Who shall I say requires him?" I thought I saw a faint smirk as these overly polite words tripped awkwardly from his lips.

"His wife, thank you." Mummy courteously replied. The young man's spotty face flushed, he said "Of course" and scuttled off. We walked around a small part of a huge space looking at the sumptuous stacks of cushions and rolls of fabric and bindings that were arrayed in an ordered fashion on wooden shelving. It was so hot in there and there were no proper windows. Ceiling fans moved the warm air around making an electronic humming as they did so, as did the fluorescent strip lighting. The lift was pinging contributing to the low-level background noise. There was a nice smell and I was keen to absorb the details of this unusual environment, but Michael seemed less interested and he was making it clear that to him what they had on sale here was really very boring. Suddenly from a concealed door which had been wallpapered and painted the same creamy colour as the walls, emerged our father. He was dressed in his usual smart work attire and was slightly red in the face but surprisingly he did look particularly delighted to see us.

"Well that's nice. I don't get many visitors." He beamed, reaching down to ruffle Michael's hair. Michael looked up and gave a cautious half smile as Daddy took his little hand and lead us forward further into the unfamiliar world of his shop floor.

"Let Dad the Bad give you all a tour. Welcome to the exotic world of soft furnishings!" He laughed and once again beamed around at us all. Despite myself I did feel slightly intrigued. Is this what he did all day, selling bits of curtain fabric and matching plump cushions to old ladies? Daddy proudly positioned himself behind a huge long narrow table with measurements marked down one side on a brass strip. Tidily organised on this, carefully positioned in built-in compartments were other tape measures, chalk, a sharp looking pair of huge black scissors and some pinking shears. There was also a dark wooden pot full of safety pins and an old-fashioned pin cushion pricked with needles and pins of many sizes and thicknesses.

"This is the cutting table. Very important area." He said in a serious voice. It all looked a bit technical for someone like my Dad to be able to manage but apparently he was the department head. He looked very comfortable behind this magnificent piece of furniture and he seemed very happy to have us in his world. He looked across the expanse of the shop floor and beckoned over the youth who had welcomed us when we first came out of the lift – "Graham, this is my family, my wife Julie and my beautiful children Samantha and Michael. Graham is our Junior Salesman. Gilbert!" he called out across the shop floor to an older chap at a cash desk in the far corner.

"Gilbert is our Senior Salesman. Been with Hartleys for many a long year." He told us. "Come, come over and meet my kids" a much older man wearing silver rimmed glasses, with a tape measure on his shoulders slowly made his way over and told us how pleased he was to meet us and that he had heard so much about us. He had a croaky voice and was crumpled and crinkly like Nanna.

Daddy let Gilbert help me and Michael to chalk some shape outlines onto material and then cut them out with the pinking shears. He watched us smiling as he spoke to Mummy. She put a shoe box on the end of the cutting table and opened it to show him the shoes she had got for Michael for school in September. He was nodding and seemed to approve of her choice.

The collars of his brown suit were wide as was his biscuit coloured tie. All the staff were dressed smartly in suits. I could see several of them dotted around the large space as I took a moment to better observe the scene now that it was Michael's turn to use the special scissors. Quietly through the door that matched the wall, the one that Daddy had come out of earlier, head high and make-up immaculate, appeared Aunty Rita. She moved slowly but decisively as if walking onto a stage set in an am dram production. She was elegantly smart in a well-cut brown pin stripe trouser suit over a beautiful cream blouse which had a frilly scarf thing attached to it at the collar and chest. She was wearing a lot of make-up and her hair was set into a shape that meant it did not move even when her head did. I could smell her perfume coming towards us in deep pungent wafts before she did.

I tensed and I am sure I felt Mummy, Daddy and Michael tense too. But she just floated past us perfectly pleasantly, saying, "Hello, nice to see you all again" as she drifted off to talk to young Graham and then set about serving the customer he was talking to.

Aunty Rita was the very opposite of my Mum who had natural beauty and a young fresh style. It was clear Mummy was flustered by her sophisticated appearance. Though of course she had known Rita worked here and inevitably would be here. Maybe that was even the reason she had wanted us all to come today. Rita oozed confidence, even authority as she glided comfortably along the shop floor on her very high heels.

Dad went quiet but only for a moment and then he regained his composure.

"How about I show you the staff canteen? There's sure to be a couple of iced buns going spare" We followed him into the lift and through some corridors and me and Michael were given cake and squash by a nice lady in an overall. Him and Mum had a coffee and then he walked us all back down the wide stairs to the entrance. He cordially thanked us for coming as though we were distant relatives he hadn't seen in years. Then he remembered himself and gave Mummy a peck on the top of the head and said, "so long kids. See you later."

Mummy was very quiet on the bus journey home. We all were and as I thought back to the visit to Daddy's shop and the people he worked with I experienced a flash of realisation- Daddy and Rita were wearing coordinated suits - his and hers versions of the same business-like brown and cream look. I digested this and thought about Sindy and Action Man. Daddy and Rita had clearly been dressed by the same person.

Once back home Mummy got us changed out of our tidy clothes and ushered us out to play very quickly. No sooner were we out on the green with the other children than I saw several Aunties rushing round to our house. Aunty Shirley had her hair in rollers with a silky scarf partially covering it all. Lit fags in hand all of them. Aunty Shirley was also carrying a bottle of something.

"Can we play jacks in my garden, I am bored with rounders tonight?" I said to Tammy and Dawn. The green was a swarm of kids on bases trying to catch each other out. The whole thing felt too energetic for me. Michael was great at rounders but he must have felt tired too because he was sprawled on the adjacent pavement playing marbles again with the littler boys. The girls wanted to stay and play on the green, so I wandered back to our front gate and sat on the steps listening to the noise and keeping an eye on Michael.

Cackling sounds and cigarette smoke drifted from the open front room window and I wondered whether or not to risk moving nearer to get a better listen. However, I reluctantly stayed on the steps not letting Michael out of the line of my view. Miraculously Michael and Robert came running up to our gate.

He had found a slow worm and had wanted to show me. I made him come closer to the window so we could look at it in the light. It was gorgeous. Bronze and shimmering. We sat on the lawn a few yards in front of the window and took turns to hold it. The boys were in awe. They laid on their little tummies in the grass and made runs for it out of sticks and leaves. My ears were burning to hear what the Aunties were saying but I couldn't hear much. There was music playing as well now so I could only get snatches of phrases and words. But the words I did catch bounced around the inside of my brain. They rattled in my head as I tried to distract Michael and prevent him from listening too.

"Slut!" one of the Aunties spat vehemently. That was the first time I ever heard a woman say that word. It felt ugly and powerful. "Who does she think she is?" someone else asked. "cradle snatcher" sounded like Aunty Shirley's voice "Brenda says her son's in trouble with the law" "AND I heard a rumour about her having a pregnant teenage daughter". The snipey tirade continued, it was easy to deduce who they were talking about "a face full of make-up but no emotion underneath". The gossip continued "her husband's at the end of his tether."

"infatuated idiot!" and finally "well she's not a patch on you Julie"

I felt pained at my Mum's sad tone as she asked, "Do you really think it's serious Shirley? Perhaps they are just friends as Brian says? I really don't know what to think anymore."

CHAPTER EIGHTEEN

The next day after work Mummy took us on a bus again, this time to Loxwood to get my new school shoes. The town seemed to be full of other mothers doing more or less the same.

"The summer's going so fast" she said, "Only a fortnight and you will both be back at school. At least the weather has been glorious. Though I don't know how much longer it can last." My mother was one of the only adults that hadn't complained once about the unceasing incredibly hot weather. She took the heat and the water shortages in her stride, using the washing up water to flush the toilet or to water her flower beds. Drenching her offspring in olive oil and vinegar and exposing us to the sun's hottest rays every chance she could. She even put lemon juice in mine and Michaels hair to make sure this unusual burst of sunshine helped her to preserve our blondness. Never once did my Mummy moan about the flying ants or sunburn or being too hot. She loved it and so did we.

It seemed funny to try on proper shoes when I had been in my Scholls for months. The days still felt lovely and hot but the evenings were a smidge cooler than they had been at the start of the holidays. It was hard to believe this warmth and freedom would come to its inevitable end and that Autumn was around the corner.

The shopping centre had been claustrophobic and muggy. Michael and I were glad to get off the bus and get home so we could go out to play. Mummy reminded us that tea would be early today as I had Brownies. We were going to do a run through of the gang show. A proper rehearsal but without the costumes. Michael was going to go for tea at Roberts because Mummy was going to go down The Woodsman with Daddy and Aunty Shirley and Uncle Sandy for a quick drink. Mum rarely went to the pub with Daddy and she seemed excited.

I put my Brownie uniform on, rolling up my long sleeves as a concession to the heat but neckerchief and beret still neatly in place. Dawn, Tammy and Jackie all came together to call for me after my tea. We wandered very slowly up to the chapel in the days lingering heat and though we were flagging when we reached the top of the hill once inside the chapel's hall we were revived by our enthusiasm and excitement for the show and somehow we threw ourselves into passionate renditions of all the songs.

Brown Owl beamed with pride. A few people had to have another go at their solos. I felt very shy when I did my little bit about the candy shop and peppermint bay but the grown ups seemed happy with it and I was spared a second go tonight.

All of us girls were given squash and biscuits at the end. Next week was full run through because the Cubs, Scouts and Guides were going to come along and add in their bits. It was going to be quite a show! What would Nanna think and Granny and Grandad from all the way across the other side of the country?

I picked Michael up from Roberts' house on my way home and Mummy was just back when we got in. She had make-up on and she looked lovely. She seemed soft around the edges and relaxed.

"Did you have a nice time Mummy?" I asked.

"Yes, thank you, very nice. It was busy down there tonight so I left your Dad there as it was his round!" I didn't know what that meant but was glad that she had had enjoyed herself and that Daddy was out. We got ready for bed and all got under the covers together in Michaels room for a quick story before sleep. She read us the Ugly Duckling because it was one of Michaels favourites.

I fell asleep almost as soon as my head hit my own pillow. It had been a tiring day.

Later through my semi conscious sleepy state I hazily perceived my father return. The noisy bang of the front door leaving the letter box rattling for a few seconds afterward followed by a drunken stumble into the front room. Some low voices. Although not fully awake I teetered on the edge of sleep, keeping myself semi awake, waiting to see if any arguing erupted. But no, things were quiet. Daddy must have been in a good mood or have fallen asleep on the sofa. I heard Mummy come quietly upstairs and into her own room to bed. All was calm.

The next morning Michael and I were at the breakfast table having our Weetabix when Aunty Shirley knocked on the back door quite aggressively. I opened it and told her that Mummy was upstairs getting dressed. She stubbed out her cigarette on the outside kitchen windowsill and marched straight in.

"Julie, Julie are you alright?"

"Morning Shirl, yes I am. Why, what's the matter?"

"I've just spoken to Brenda at the pub."

"O yes? Is everything alright? O don't tell me Brian didn't pay for his round?"

"No, well I know I don't know about that, probably not, but that's not what I mean. No. What I mean is that it seems there was a bit of bother with your Brian after we all left the pub last night."

They had both gone into the front room and I could feel Mummy's morning mood deflate as they sat down on the sofa. Aunty Shirley was bursting with the excitement due to whatever information she had gleaned from Brenda the bar lady at The Woodsman. I turned off Elton John and Kiki Dee's nauseating chirping at each other on the radio so that I could get a better listen.

"Apparently your Brian and Kevin had quite a ding-dong!"

"What? What do you mean Shirley?" Mum looked at her slightly disbelievingly. "Brian never mentioned anything when he came in last night!"

"Well, according to Brenda, Kevin gave Brian a piece of his mind and Brian gave him something back. Des and Tom had to get between them."

"O no this must be a mistake. Surely? Brian would have said something"

"Well I am sure Kevin will tell you everything when you go down to work later. It seems there was quite a set to between them." Mum gasped but she was not ready for Aunty Shirley's denouement…

"and it's not like Kevin could hide it even if he wanted to with the whopping black eye your Brian gave him for everyone to see!"

Mum gasped. Now she had said her piece Aunty Shirley stood up to her full height and got ready to leave. She was strikingly tall and lanky and she looked resplendent at having accomplished her news bearing so effectively.

"A black eye? Are you sure?"

"Well that's what Brenda says Julie. You know all about your Brian and black eyes don't you?"

She had gone too far. Neither of them spoke. Shaky silence then the sound of a cigarette packet being opened. My eyes returned to my Weetabix bowl but they both must have taken one as Shirley lit each cigarette then inhaled and exhaled deeply and loudly. Still no reply from my Mummy. I looked into the living room and could only see her sitting inside. Very still, just holding the cigarette in her hand but not smoking it.

"Well I must be getting on." Aunty Shirley said awkwardly as she came back towards us and strode through the kitchen towards the back door. "Samantha, I am taking Dawn and

Andrew to the Lido later if you would like to come along with us when your Mum gets back from work?" she raised a highly plucked eyebrow and glared down at me as she made this offer.

I was dumbfounded and just nodded at her as she marched past me and Michael still sat at the kitchen table. She headed to the backdoor,

"See you later Julie" she said more softly and she exited the scene she had created. Mummy had followed her into the kitchen and looked at us. She smiled, slightly bemused.

"Don't take any notice of your Aunty Shirley. Now eat up both of you."

Me and Michael looked at each other and then ate. I fully believed Dad would have hit fat Kevin given the very slightest provocation. Michael evidently did too as I saw a happy little smirk appear on his lips.

"I am just popping over the road to speak with Aunty Beryl a moment. Make sure you both clear the dishes and wash up when you've had enough." And then she left through the back door too. A second later she poked her head back in, "and don't go out to play until I get back!"

We did as instructed. She was a little flustered when she got back not that long afterwards.

"Now kids, Aunty Beryl says you can go round to hers for a little while this morning so that I can go down to work a bit earlier than usual."

"O no Mum, it's boring round there." said Michael in a whiny voice. I wasn't that bothered really. Aunty Beryl always had nice sweets because Karen bought them home from the sweet shop. Karen had a nice dolls house too from when she was a little girl that I would be allowed to play with.

"Uncle Tom says you can help him build a little kennel for Tinkerbelle" that sold it, Michael went upstairs to get his little toolbox and we were ready. Because Aunty Beryl was older than the other aunties she was calmer and kinder and we had such a nice morning. Mummy seemed fine when she came home from work and I did go to the Lido with Dawn's family and the day flashed by in a rush.

At teatime though Daddy didn't come home at his usual time. Michael went out into the back garden to clean out Herbert but he came back a few moments later pale and then burst into tears. He flung himself at Mummy and he sobbed and told her that Herbert was dead.

Mummy looked disbelieving. She held him firmly and kissed and consoled him then went out to take a look saying

"Both of you stay inside"

"Perhaps he's just sleeping." I said to Michael.

"Sleeping with a cord around his neck. I don't think so!" Michael snapped nastily. He had stopped sobbing now.

"A cord?"

"Looks like clothesline or something." He mumbled. From the colour of her skin and the look on Mummy's face when she came back in a few moments later it was clear that Herbert was indeed dead. I burst into uncontrollable tears even though the little thing was not at all that dear to me. It just felt so shocking. He was such a harmless yet fragile creature.

"Michael says he was strangled with a cord" I whimpered.

"It looks like some kind of, of nasty accident." she said gently, her own eyes now also full of tears at the sight of both her children crying.

"Accident? How can it be an acc…." Michael began but then was crying so strongly that he couldn't finish his sentence.

"I will ask uncle Ed to come and bury him in the morning. Please neither of you go out there til that's done." We were sobbing so much that we couldn't answer her but of course, neither of us did.

CHAPTER NINETEEN

The space where the hutch had been was completely cleared away and no trace of it or Herbert remained the next day when Michael and I went out to play. I asked Mummy if Herbert had gone to heaven and she said yes and that he would see his guinea pig family there and be happy. I felt vaguely satisfied with this and anyway we all had other things on our minds.

Daddy hadn't come home from work since the evening after the night at the pub when he hit Uncle Kevin. That was three nights ago now and Nanna had come round to help Mummy and find out what had happened. Mummy told Nanna that she had phoned Hartley's and Dad's boss there had told her that Mr Reid had gone on annual leave and they weren't expecting him back for ten days. They both seemed relieved that at least he hadn't lost yet another job.

"He'll be with HER." Mummy said matter of factley to Nanna and Nanna couldn't even be bothered to argue against this likelihood. She just shook her head sadly. They were talking whilst Nanna pinned the fancy collar onto my Shirley Temple dress as I stood on a kitchen chair wearing it. I had to keep very still so that she could get the positioning just right.

"I don't know what to say Julie but I am praying for you all every night." Was all Nanna could offer. She said she'd stay and do a jigsaw with us kids whilst Mummy went down to work at the chip shop. Daddy hadn't left her any housekeeping money so she was now having to do evening shifts as well as lunchtimes to get by.

"If it wasn't for Kevin we would be out on the streets now Gwen, thanks to your son"

"I'd never let that happen Julie. You know you could all come back and live with me again." Mum burst out laughing but then it turned into crying. Heavy heartfelt sobs.

"How could he do this to us? How? Everyone knows, it's so humiliating. I hate that woman! I hate Brian"

Nanna couldn't stay every evening, she had things to do at her Chapel so sometimes Mummy had to put us to bed early and leave us on our own whilst she went to work. She looked exhausted and washed out. There was not time for cooking so she bought us home lots of chips that week.

Nanna came back on the Friday to see if Daddy had returned. He had not and there had been no word from him. Mummy had been down the pub to ask his friends if they knew where he was but she said they were clueless.

Mummy asked Nanna to stay with us through that afternoon between her shifts as she had decided to go and see Aunty Rita's husband to find out if he knew where they were. She assumed that they must be together because Aunty Shirley had rung the shop asking for her and had been told that she too was off on holiday.

Between shifts, whilst Nanna looked after us Mummy caught the bus over to the other side of Loxwood to the smarter part of town called Norton where Aunty Rita lived with her husband Tony. Mummy looked drawn and anxious as she left us and told us to be good children for Nanna.

"Are you sure this is a good idea Julie?" Nanna asked her. "There could be an innocent explanation"

Mum said nothing and left in a decisive manner.

It felt to me like she was gone a long time but a few hours later she returned. Mummy was rarely angry but you could see that she was fuming. She even slammed the front door shut behind her, something she never did. Michael was in the back garden digging a hole and probably eating mud. I was just sitting down near the back window watching him and reading one of my boarding schoolbooks whilst Nanna sewed.

Mummy threw her beaded hessian bag down and then slammed the living room door behind her too for extra effect. I felt total trepidation and Nanna looked very anxious as well.

"Well Gwen" Mummy started. "Here is your totally innocent explanation as to the whereabouts of your only son. It seems that he and Rita have been having an affair for over 6 months that Tony knows about at any rate, but maybe much longer. That's why they are separated, Rita and Tony, because of Brian. Tony confronted them. She refused to give Brian up" Nanna gasped, they both ignored me. I kept still and quiet in the corner.

"Apparently, they say that they are the loves of each others lives!" another gasp from Nanna.

"But that's not the best bit Gwen, O no. Whilst I work my fingers to the bone and bring up his children and keep a home, whilst I am stinking of greasy fish and chips and trying to keep a roof over his children's head, do you know, do you have any idea of where your precious son is? Right now. Right this minute. Do you?" Mum almost shouted the last bit and this was so out of character that I felt the tears start to well up in my eyes.

"No Julie, you know I don't" Nanna's voice was meek.

"Well let me just enlighten you. He's probably guzzling Spanish beer on a sun lounger near a pool because Brian is, at this minute, enjoying a luxury package holiday in sunny Spain with his bloody mistress! The love of his bloody life! That's where he is." Mum sobbed, turned on her heels and ran upstairs to the bedroom.

Michael was concentrating on digging and it seemed that he couldn't have heard any of this. I was still invisible to Nanna. She was ashen. She stood up and straightened her dress with her hands, slowly and methodically. Then she put her head up and seemed to sleepwalk straight past me to the kitchen. I heard her fill the kettle and put it on the stove as she started to make a pot of tea.

A few moments after, with unnerving timing, Aunty Shirley walked straight in through the back door as if this was her own house. She calmly took a cup of tea out of Nannas' hands and carried it upstairs to my Mummy. Nanna didn't flinch she just stood there looking out the window at Michael in the garden in the hot sunshine playing by himself. She looked dazed.

I felt a bit dazed myself. Was this all my fault? Was this God answering my prayer? Had Daddy gone forever? Could it be possible?

Just to make sure, I quickly recited in my head, "Please God, please, please God, please don't let him come back. Ever. Amen"

CHAPTER TWENTY

"He's broken my heart Shirl. He promised he wouldn't and he has. How could he do this? He said he would take us to Spain, his wife, his children, his family and he's gone off there, buggered off there with HER!"

"I'm sorry Julie. I don't like to say I told you so."

"Well don't then. I still can't believe it. Her husband is in pieces. He's quite elderly, not in the best of health. The poor bloke is devastated. Their whole family is a worse mess than ours. Her son is 18 and is due in court next week for stealing cars. He could go down and she's in bloody Spain. What kind of a mother, what kind of a person is she?"

"Not a patch on you Julie"

"And it's all true about her daughter. Poor young thing. She is pregnant. Sixteen years of age and expecting a baby. Living with her boyfriend and his family. Her own Mum not speaking to her, gallivanting around Spain with her toy boy boyfriend, my husband......"

I knocked on the bedroom door and poked my head round. "Nanna says would you like her to make us some tea and would you like something to eat before you go back to work?"

"Um could you ask her to do you those fish fingers and there's some tinned spaghetti? Not for me though. I am not hungry." Mummy looked so sad. I went over and cuddled into her. Aunty Shirley sat stiffly on the edge of the bed.

Mum patted my hair and then pulled herself up.

"I need to hurry up and get changed to get ready for work. Friday is always a busy night." She said trying to sound breezy.

"Yes I suppose I better go home and get my own kids their tea as well" Aunty Shirley said.

"I've got a nice Arctic roll in the freezer. I'll send it round with Andrew and you and Michael can have that for your pudding" she said to me.

"Thanks Shirl." Mum said, "Tell Nanna I'll be down in a few minutes Spangle." I made my way out slowly, hoping for a few more scraps of information.

"Sorry Julie, you are probably still in shock. Do you think you should be going into work tonight?"

"The milkman needs paying. The electric bill is overdue. There's hardly any food in this house. I'm penniless. I've got no choice Shirley. Anyway it'll take my mind off things for a bit. I'll see if Gwen can stay with the kids."

"Kevin will understand. He knows. I think he's friendly with Tony. He's got family himself in Norton and he'd heard things. I expect that's why he confronted your Brian." She tried to say this in a kind voice but Mummy's face twisted.

"O no, how humiliating. And that hurts, everyone knowing. Did everyone except me know?" Mum said quietly with a sob in her voice and I felt pained too and guilty for knowing and I hurried away back downstairs.

CHAPTER TWENTY ONE

For the whole of the next day the house was awash with a stream of Aunties toing and froing offering advice, making tea and coffee, offering help and bringing packets of fags and tins of groceries as payment for each new bit of gossip they gleaned from my poor mother.

Kevin had also come to the house earlier and had given Mummy the day off, with pay, because he said he was worried about her health.

"Call it sick pay, Julie. After all you are a valued member of staff at Fryer Tucks."

He sounded very business-like and important but he looked young and awkward even to my eyes. He was wearing his immaculate white cotton chip shop overalls and he was sweating a lot. He still had the trace of a black eye but said he would pop up again on Monday to see how she was. He also said that he had spoken to Tony and that Rita and Brian were scheduled to fly home next Wednesday. He told Mum that he was "there for her." gave her a meaningful look and left.

Nanna went home. She said she needed to speak to her minister. She was in turmoil and the atmosphere between her and Mummy was tense. They were barely speaking. It was still terribly hot and everything had become dramatic and heady.

I would not venture further than the garden and was keeping a very tight rein on Michael who seemed to instinctively know that he had to behave and keep his head down and stay close to me. That afternoon the flying ants came out and we both went inside for some shade.

It was cooler and more peaceful than earlier. The only Aunty still there was Beryl. She had soft short brown curly hair flecked with grey and a crinkly face with thick lensed spectacles. She had on a sensible summer dress, old fashioned with buttons and covered in roses. On her feet she wore sturdy Clarke's sandals. No platforms, short shorts or gaudy nail varnish like Aunty Shirley. No dyed hair like Aunty Doreen. No expensive fashionable clothes like Aunty Janice. No cigarettes either. She was nicer and more sensible than the others and I could see she was having a calming effect on my Mummy.

Mummy looked tear stained and washed out. She put out her cigarette in the ashtray between them on the kitchen table. She was still dressed in her housecoat and slippers. Her long brown hair was lank around her face.

"You must take your time and follow your own heart Julie." She said kindly.

"This is your life and not someone else's. It's not a story or something on the telly."

"That's how it feels at the moment." Mum said.

"I know. You've got a few days breathing space now. To quietly think about things and think about what is best for you and the children."

"Yes" Mum looked tired.

"It's such a mess Doreen. Holidays have to be booked and planned in advance so he must have known he was going away. He must have packed things to take. All the time acting as if everything was fine. And the cost of it! He would never spend an amount of money like that on us. He denied anything was going on and I wanted to trust him. He's a liar and a cheat" she was getting herself all worked up again.

"Ssshhh now. None of that can be changed."

"So selfish"

"People can be"

128

"He's always been restless. I know that. But I don't want much Beryl. I just wanted us to be like a normal family."

I looked at Michael asleep on the sofa beside me. His cheeks were flushed and he looked sweet. It was so hot I could have dozed off myself. I was pretending to read my book but I could sense Mummy look at me so I turned to face her through the kitchen door and I gave her a smile.

"Well now, there's no such thing as that now is there?" Beryl smiled and took Mummy's hand.

"You are a lovely young woman and your life is just beginning. You can make your own choices. When you're ready."

"I know what's important at any rate." Mummy said warmly and she smiled at me and Michael.

The next day Mummy dressed us up smartly in our Sunday best and took us up to Chapel. She had asked Aunty Beryl to ring Nanna's minister and he had made sure that she was there at our Chapel for the service as well. We all sat together. I was glad to see that they were friends again. The sun shone brightly through the murky green windows but it was cool in the concrete cavern of the modern building. It was like being in cool water, fully dressed, in your best clothes.

The Sunday service was so boring and so long. I could see Michael couldn't take much more of it but thankfully, finally the last prayer ended, the Minister blessed us all and we could go outside into the warmth of the sunshine.

There were loads of children in the grounds and we joined in a game of tag whilst the adults all chatted. Nanna had to catch her bus back home but she gave me and Michael extra tight hugs and I felt the bristles from her moustache dig into my cheeks when she kissed me goodbye. Then I saw her push some pound notes into Mummy's hand and brush away a tiny tear.

In that small moment my own heart froze for it was plain to see that both their hearts were broken. That's what my Daddy had done to them. For all his faults they had loved him and he had broken their hearts.

CHAPTER TWENTY TWO

Mummy went back to work at the chip shop on Monday. I went to Brownies as usual that evening and Michael stayed over at Aunty Beryl's and Uncle Toms until I got back. Then Aunty Beryl came to sit with us until my Mummy finished work.

The next day we had a nice surprise because Aunty Cathy came and she took me and Michael to the zoo which was quite a long way on a bumpy coach that we caught in town. Once through the ornate zoo gates it was hot and crowded but we joined the throng and made our way around the cages and enclosures. The gardens were impressive, if a bit wilted because of the heatwave but there was an elephant having a shower with a hose pipe which was such a happy sight to see. Aunty Cathy laughed at the peculiarity and she blushed when the zookeeper pretended to throw his bucket of water at her.

It was kind of her to take us. Aunty Cathy wore a pretty powder blue cotton dress and her smile was kind and joyful. No wonder the zookeeper noticed her. She was shy but she stood out. We strolled around quietly and we all enjoyed the chimpanzees even if you could hardly see them because there were so many people all trying to get close to them at the same time. We each had a sausage roll for lunch that she had bought with her in a brown paper bag. She also bought us a souvenir to take home from the gift shop which was a pencil each with a different animal as the rubber on the end. I had an elephant as it was my favourite animal and Michael had a little monkey which I thought was apt.

Then it was the Wednesday, the day that Daddy was due back home from his holiday in Spain. We all felt anxious but did not speak about it. Nanna came to our house in the morning and Mummy went to work at lunchtime as usual. In the evening he was still not home and Nanna was staying over so Mummy went back into work again. But in the end Daddy didn't come home that evening after all.

I was glad, but I felt very tense. What if he did? Would there be more arguing and fighting? I had a horrible nervous stomach ache. Michael appeared to be his usual quiet self and he had spent most of the day playing with his cars under the porch with Robert. They had put an old blanket on the metal frame to make it like a tent and they had constructed a little town in there to position and move their toy vehicles in. They were quietly and happily engrossed only stopping to eat their sandwich spread sandwiches which Nanna bought out for them.

Nanna had decided to stay again on the Thursday to help Mum and 'provide moral support.' By this time my stomach ache was quite fierce and I could only lie on the sofa feeling very unwell. Mum put her hand on my forehead to see if I had a temperature. My tummy was in knots but I told her to go to work and I would be fine here with Nanna. She looked worried and spoke quietly to Nanna in the kitchen. Then she came back in and said that she would bring me home some Lucozade and that I should try and get some sleep. I nodded feebly and closed my eyes and off she went.

Nanna and Michael were at the table together doing a puzzle and I must have dozed off because when I woke up Mummy was home again and the day was drawing in.

"I've told Kevin I'll not work tonight. Not with Spangle so poorly." I heard her telling Nanna.

"If you want to go back home we will be fine."

"I don't know what to do for the best Julie" Nanna replied. At that very moment we heard what could only be the sound of Dad's key in the lock of the front door. Each one of us froze and I felt physically sick. I realised just how frightened I was of him and from Michaels face I could see he felt the same.

The time it took for him to walk down the hall to the sitting room door felt like an age. Then, he poked his cocky sun-tanned head round the door and cracked a smile at the four of our startled faces.

"Ola! It's Dad the Bad" he winked, "Did you all miss me?"

I looked at Mummy's face. She looked at Nanna.

"Brian" Nanna said but then words seemed to totally fail her.

"Alright Mother? Your bad penny returns." he said marching in a bit bolder now and planting a rough kiss on Nannas' cheek.

"I bet you all can't wait to see what souvenirs I brought you all back from sunny Espania!" that was the straw that broke Mummy's back. She stood up and faced him.

"If you have come back for your things Brian, I have saved you some time and packed a bag for you. It's by the bedroom door."

Silence, shifting of weight from one foot to the other.

"Come on now Julie" he said softly. "No need for that. No need to overreact. I just needed a little break away from it all. A man's only human. I came back didn't I?" he laughed.

"Please don't take too long Brian. Spangle is not well and I need to get the kids to bed. I am sure Rita is waiting for you."

At the mention of Rita's name Michael suddenly started to cry. Dad sneered,

"I told you you were turning that boy into a bloody sissy." He pointed his finger nastily at Mummy's face. Michael cried louder.

"Go Brian please" Mummy implored him.

Dad was clearly thinking through the best strategy to deploy for this situation. Nanna stood up and said, "You've done enough damage for one day Brian I think you should go now please."

Daddy became furious, "Look what you've done you bloody bitch, turned my own Mother against me. Bloody kids are too bloody soft because of you. Sons a bloody fairy!" He was still pointing and edging closer to her, his finger almost within touching distance of Mummy's face.

"That's enough! Are you drunk Brian?" Nanna squared up to him.

"I might have had a drop of the ol' duty free" he laughed. He looked at each one of us. He was not shamefaced, though a bit wobbly on his feet. There was a stern silence directed at him by both women.

"I guess I know where I'm not wanted. So I'll go for tonight. I'll not take that bag though. I'll be back tomorrow, back in my own home where I belong. My names on the rent book Julie and don't you bloody forget it. This is my house, my family and I'm not going anywhere"

He turned on his heel.

"You know what? You'll all be begging me to come back." he added.

"Not whilst you're seeing another woman I won't Brian. Don't cross this threshold."

He moved jerkily towards her his hand raised, angry, ready to slap her as he had done so many times before. The dark brown room felt more oppressive than ever.

"No" I shouted

"No Brian. Leave. That's enough I say." said Nanna firmly taking a step towards him. He backed out of the room, bending down to pick up his Spanish carrier bag.

"Adios!" he sneered. "Don't cry kids. Daddy'll be back soon." He said cheerily. He gave a wave of his hand and went backwards out the way he had come in, reversing down the hall.

Nanna followed him and put the bolt across the door after checking it was properly shut. She looked shaken when she came back into the living room, but she went out to the kitchen and bolted the back door too and then put the kettle on.

Michael had moved over to the front room window. He was watching Daddy saunter off down the street. Some of the neighbours were probably doing the same thing through their own windows. Daddy must have raised his hand in a defiant wave as I caught Michael lift his own little hand to wave back. He sighed as he caught me watching him. I went over and pulled the curtains closed and did the same for the ones at the back window. I turned the lamp on.

Mummy slumped down in the sofa. She wasn't crying now but she did look fraught, her mind racing with competing thoughts.

"My Harold must be turning in his grave. I thank God that his father is not alive to see Brian behaving in such a way."

"What am I to do Gwen? He's got no shame at all. What on earth am I to do?"

"I don't know Julie dear. I'm sorry."

"What if he won't leave. Would he put us out on the streets?"

"It won't come to that. Perhaps he's seeing the error of his ways. He wants you back Julie."

"No Gwen. No he doesn't. He wants his cake and eat it. The bastard thinks he's done nothing wrong. Sorry kids." She blushed at the swear word not realising we had just heard far worse.

"I don't understand where he gets it from. His father was a gentle soul. Respectful. He'll be turning in his grave Julie. Let's see if we can find something on the box to watch and have a nice cup of tea shall we?" Nanna suggested. "Julie. Perhaps you could talk to the minister about finding forgiveness?"

"Forgiveness? No. I don't think so Gwen. No tea for me." Mummy over to the sideboard and took out a brown bottle of Sherry. She poured some into a fine tumbler and swigged it. Then she switched the telly on.

"You can watch Top of the Pops kids and then it's bed." She topped up her glass and sat down with us.

"It's a solicitor I need to talk to not the minister. Only I can't afford to. Funny how Brian is swimming in money and his wife and kids can't afford the basics." She took another sip of her drink.

"Don't think like that Julie. I am sure we could get him to change. Perhaps the minister could talk to Brian" Mum laughed so hard that some of the sherry shot out of her mouth.

"That's a conversation I'd like to be a fly on the wall for! Stop kidding yourself Gwen."

The Real Thing started singing "you to me are everything, the sweetest song that I could sing O baby" and I saw tears begin to well up in Mummy's eyes. I snuggled into her, "to you I guess I'm just a clown who picks you up each time you're down O baby" she hugged me back tightly. "You give me just a taste of love to build my hopes upon, you know you've got the power boy to keep me hanging on" She downed the rest of her glass.

"He's doesn't even know what love is" Mummy said as a very ugly man with a cigar and a track suit announced the next song – "You'll never find another love like mine" by Lou Rawls.

"He never will either. I hope she's worth it" said Mum and went back to the sideboard for more sherry.

CHAPTER TWENTY THREE

Daddy came round the next day after work and he quietly took his packed bag and went away again. Before he went he gave me a pair of castanets wrapped in yellow tissue paper and Michael a little plastic bullfighter on a stand next to a plastic bull. I don't think either of us knew what to make of this. He was in self-pitying mode, calling himself Dad the Bad and looked sad and even had tears in his eyes but he didn't stay long.

Mummy said nothing until he was completely out of the door and then she opened it again and shouted "and don't come back!" and then slammed it shut and locked it with the bolt. Although he didn't come back that day he did come back the next day but they started arguing soon afterwards and Aunty Beryl and Uncle Tom came over and then Daddy left. Michael and I were outside playing and I saw this from across the road by the ladybird bushes where a few of us were playing jacks in the shade.

I was starting to look forward to going back to school and to getting some kind of normality and routine back into our lives. This tension and uncertainty was horrible and felt more public and exposed than ever before. The gang show was to be next Sunday then we would have two more days off for the Bank Holiday and then it would be school! The endless summer was coming to its end. August creeping to its close. It's crazy heat and our family drama had been exhausting.

Mummy was looking thinner, paler and more bewildered by the day. Nanna had gone home again to go to her own chapel to ask her minister for guidance.

The aunties came and went in an ad-hoc fashion. They now seemed more measured and careful about what they said and they spoke in quieter voices than before. Though Aunty Shirley could not contain her excitement one evening when she came over with a copy of the local paper. Her voice escalated as she read aloud a small paragraph of text she had previously encircled in biro. "Martin Ravello, aged 19, of 37, Ash Leighs, Norton, Loxwood was today sentenced by magistrates to six months in prison for theft of a motor vehicle, driving without a license, exceeding the speed limit and driving in a reckless fashion. The magistrates told the court they had shown leniency on Ravello because he had come from a broken home."

Aunty Shirley clearly relished the reading of this.

"Broken home! Humpf ! Wonder if Mommy Dearest was there in the court to hold his hand?" she snorted. Mummy though clearly took no pleasure in this.

"It can't have been easy for any of them I don't suppose. Even Rita." She said quietly. "A boy of that age in prison. Poor Tony." She shook her head to the offer of the newspaper as Aunty Shirley thrust it in her direction.

That Sunday was another superhot day. Balmy in fact and Mummy dressed us both in denim shorts and blue cotton short sleeved shirts that matched. After breakfast we played in the garden together for a while in a tent made out of an old blanket but just before lunch I noticed Gary and Phillip were outside our house on their bikes. They wanted to know if any gang members wanted to bike it down to the swing park for a picnic. A few of the kids had started to assemble around them with their duffle bags.

"Come on Michael, let's ask Mum if we can take a picnic and go with them" I said. It would be good to get away from Sycamore Drive for a while.

Mummy gladly made us some sandwiches and put them in a Tupperware with some Dairylea cheese triangles and an apple each. She also gave us a bag of broken biscuits she had bought from the factory shop to share with the others. She told us to be good and to be back in time for tea. Although there was no specified time for this we somehow always seemed to know exactly when it was so I promised that we would and we joined the others.

Although the swing park can't have been much more than a mile away from our street it gave us some distance and it felt nice to be out of sight of all the misery and oppression for a few hours.

Michael was doing wheelies on his bike at the front of our gang's convoy. He was really rather dextrous. He was in his element as some of the big boys cheered him on. Jackie, Stacey, Tammy and me were towards the back of the pack and were coasting down the gentle hill to the flat river plain where the swing park was situated. We all turned off the road and onto the public bridleways which criss-crossed the fields down to the river and the swing park that sat beside it. It felt so liberating to be away from the adults and we raced and larked around for ages before we parked up our bikes against the railings and sat down on the grass for something to eat.

We took it in turns to quench our thirsts at the water fountain and then scattered out onto the swings, slides, roundabout and monkey bars. It was a well-equipped and spacious playground and the shallow River Lox burbled past as we played.

Away from the cares of our sordid domestic life I felt so liberated and happy with my friends. Michael, Robert and another younger boy called Malcolm were trying to make some kind of craft out of some bits of wooden pallet that were on the stony beach next to the river. I was impressed by how ingenious Michael could be. He looked wide-eyed and thoughtful as they worked and chatted together. One of them cracked a joke. It was nice to see him smiling for a change.

Some of us were lying on the grassy ledge next to the beach. The sky was azure, a perfect afternoon even though it was starting to get dark earlier than previous weeks. The starlings were starting to gather on the lines joining the telegraph posts. As the sun moved down to the land the sky rippled and shimmered with vibrant, golds and silvers. It seemed close enough to draw it down and wrap around you like a gaudy silken throw. It was a sublime afternoon.

As the sun dipped lower we all knew it was time to go home and that Mothers would be getting our tea ready and keeping their eyes out for our return. I made sure I had all our rubbish and Tupperware back in my drawstring bag and went to the fountain to get a last drink. Michael was ready too and I felt pleased that he had so clearly had a nice day as well.

Gary and Phillip took to the front, most of the little ones were in the middle and me and the bigger girls were towards the back of the formation. Although it wasn't anywhere near dark, it was dusky and you needed to keep your eyes peeled even though there were very few cars about. And anyway, being a Sunday the streets were especially quiet. That's probably why none of us were expecting what happened to happen.

One moment all was calm and the next, from nowhere like an anxious buzzing bee a motorbike came up behind us. He revved a few times, anxious to overtake. But we were a messy swarm. We were spilled out across both lanes of the road and movement was erratically sideways as well as forwards. I called out

"MBC" which in our world meant motorbike coming and as Tammy called "Keep to the left" her words were lost in the engine sounds as the motorbike rider edged out past us girls to try and overtake. He hesitated, then he must have changed his mind and went back in behind us as he had failed to fully gauge the size of our group and he needed to have a rethink.

We were going uphill now and had to pedal harder so our pack inevitably slowed. We were tired and became even more straggly and for some mad reason the biker decided to pull out again and try to get past us. But as he crossed the white line

141

he clipped one of the little ones. A spin and then the child went down with a dull thud. In a moment a hideous domino effect occurred and another lost balance and tumbled on top of them. Then Jackie, who was bigger and quite heavy failed to stop in time and she fell on top of them too. Whoever was on the bottom now was being pinned to the road by two other children and their bicycles.

Of course, it was Michael.

The motor cyclist was gone. Everything was quiet and the gang was now spread over an even larger distance.

"Stop, stop" Stacey and I were calling to Gary and Phillip who were now some way ahead. The middle of the group had all stopped and they were off their bikes.

"Go and get my Mum, it's Michael, he's hurt, please someone go and get my Mum" I said. Gary immediately sprang into action and ran off up Oak Hill towards my house.

Jackie stretched herself then stood up and carefully moved her bike from the crumpled mass. Malcom was beneath moving slowly at first. It was only his leg that had really been trapped and now Jackie was up he was able to tentatively move it. Underneath him though lay Michael in his now familiar deathly pose. He looked like a stricken fawn, lifeless and innocent. His mangled bike was wrapped around one of his little legs. Sticking out of his summer shorts his legs looked like sticks.

He had a trickle of red dribbling down his forehead and I could see that there was more dark blood mated in his white angel hair.

O God no, I thought, could this really be it? Is God coming down to take him back up to heaven? After all the other accidents and dangers he had survived was this going to finally be it?

Before God had time to come and reclaim Michael a Green Morris Minor pulled up out of nowhere. I had no idea even of which direction it had come from. The driver poked his head out of the window and said, "Ay ay. What's going on here then?" very much like the policeman in Dixon of Dock Green.

It was my Dad. Cocky, smiling. Then taking in the scene properly, suddenly serious and concerned.

"Daddy. It's Michael, he's been hurt. He's been knocked over by a motor bike." My Dad got out of the car just as Mummy came running down the road.

"Michael, Michael!" she called as she got nearer.

Dad was on the floor beside him now. His face was taut with fear.

"Michael lad, are you alright Sonny Jim? Michael?" nothing. Mummy knelt down next to me and took Michaels' hand and then my hand as we both leaned in to look at his vulnerable shape on the road. She looked at him and then at me.

"Spangle are you alright?" I didn't say anything. I was not alright.

"Right" said Dad uncharacteristically taking control "Julie open the car door, backseat."

"What car door?" Mummy looked at him puzzled.

"My car woman, this car, hurry up." He said pointing at the car I had seen him kissing Aunty Rita in.

"Your car? You can't afford to give me housekeeping but you can go out and buy a car."

"Julie open the bloody car door." He now had Michael's inert body in his arms having lifted him out of the wreckage of his twisted bike.

"We need to get Michael to the hospital. Spangle, put your bag on the seat under his head. I don't want him getting any blood on my seat covers!"

Mummy had gone into shock. On top of the fact that her baby child had suffered a life-threatening accident the whole car thing was just too much. She stood up and shot Daddy a look of pure hatred but she took hold of my hand and then got into the front seat of the car placing me on her lap whilst Daddy laid Michael carefully across the back seats.

Uncle Ed came charging down to find out what had happened.

"Is everything alright Julie?" he asked ignoring Daddy. Mummy shook her head.

"I'm sorry. So sorry. Don't worry Julie. I'll report it to the police and take the kids bikes back to your house" he said all this kindly to Mummy through the car window. Dad mumbled thanks but Uncle Ed made no acknowledgment.

Daddy jumped into the driver seat, turned the ignition and sped off leaving the scattered and bruised remnants of our gang in the roadside with Uncle Ed. He was driving very fast. It was giddying. I held tightly to Mummy's hand realising it was the first and only time we had ever all been on a car journey together. Even in the awfulness of that situation and that moment I was acutely aware that, to outside eyes we gave the semblance of a normal family out and about together in their family car and I noticed that this pleased me. It would have pleased Michael even more if only he had been conscious to enjoy it.

Daddy was a good driver. His face was focused on the road ahead. He seemed very happy to be doing something to help. But Mummy was not impressed with him in any way and the journey was tense. But luckily it was a short one. Mummy said not one word as we hastened along the quiet roads to Old Loxwood to reach the local hospital with little Michael injured and unconscious on the back seat. We could all hear

144

him breathing quite noisily which was reassuring and scary at the same time.

It was starting to get dark and the lights of the hospital glowed in front of us as Daddy turned in through the old-fashioned metal gates and skidded right up in front of the emergency ward doors.

CHAPTER TWENTY FOUR

Michael was snatched from us by uniformed professionals and taken off to the mysterious hospital environs so a doctor could assess the damage. Michaels' leg was broken. He had a sprained wrist and minor head injuries. He was going to need an operation to reset his leg and he would be in and out of hospital for a while. He looked very pale and small in his metal hospital bed. He was in a lot of pain and so was on morphine and he was attached to various machines and bags of fluid. The graze on his forehead was deep and there were still small stones from the road embedded within it.

The staff at the hospital were kind and gentle with all of us. A policeman came in for a short while and talked to Mummy and Daddy. He said he would contact Mummy in the next few days.

It was very late by the time they finished checking Michael over and making him comfortable. As he was so very poorly Mummy was going to stay in overnight with him and sleep in the chair by his bed. Daddy was going to take me home and look after me. Michael would be having his operation in the morning. The hospital had let Mummy ring Aunty Cathy as she had a phone in the digs where she lived and it was all arranged that Nanna was going to come to our house in the morning so Daddy could go to work. This huge responsibility on Dad to do something useful and caring would be a first and was clearly something none of us except him, felt comfortable with.

"You dare leave her on her own and I will kill you with my bare hands." Were the last words Mummy said to him as he led me out toward his car.

"I don't know what your mother was trying to imply there, Spangle" he said as he opened the passenger side door to let me get in.

"Of course I would not leave my little girl all alone. But say, how do you fancy stopping by the pub with me for a quick one on the way home? I am sure Aunty Brenda will be able to supply you with lemonade and some crisps. You'd like that wouldn't you?" He gave a smile and a wink. "O and you'd better clunk click but I don't think I'll bother!" and we drove straight from the hospital to the Woodsman to get the last hour before closing time.

I was tired but pop and crisps were quite an incentive and anyway I hadn't had any tea. The regulars had already heard the news about poor Michaels' accident so there was no shortage of people wanting to buy Daddy a drink to get the full account. Many had ideas and suggestions about what should be done to the bike rider whose fault it was if he ever got caught and the conversation got quite raucous.

It was smoky and the pub was cosily lit with soft red lamps on the walls and at some of the tables. Everyone was friendly and welcoming and there didn't seem to be any problem with a small child being there late at night.

Daddy was loving all the attention, as well as the free drinks. They were raising their glasses and saying, "To little Michael, get well soon!" And Daddy seemed to be like some kind of hero to them all.

I was given more pop and some peanuts and when I got tired I curled up in a red leatherette bar chair and Daddy put his heavy suede jacket over me like a blanket.

I don't remember how or when wc got home and I woke up in my bed the next morning in my clothes. But I was all in one piece so hopefully Mummy wouldn't be upset about it. I heard Daddy go off to work and Nanna moving about downstairs. Tidying up and putting the kettle on.

I was washed and dressed in clean clothes by the time Mummy came back later that morning. She seemed pleased to see me and Nanna. She gave me a tight hug and I could smell the smell of hospital on her.

"My do I need a hot bath" she said. "and a change of clothes. I haven't slept a wink." Nanna put a cup of tea down in front of her and went upstairs to run her a shallow bubble bath.

At this very moment Michael was in the theatre having his operation Mummy told me before going upstairs to have her bath. An operation sounded like a very serious thing to me. I thought of the board game Dawn and Andrew had for Christmas and I wanted to know more.

When she came back downstairs dressed in clean clothes and with washed hair Mummy told us that they were going to put some pins in Michael's broken leg. They would help set the bone back into the shape it had been before it got broken by the weight of his bike landing on it. He wouldn't feel them doing it because they put you to sleep with medicine and he would be coming around at about the time she got back.

"That's why I can't stay long Spangle. I want to be there when he wakes up. But I will be back at teatime." He would have a scar and some more stiches. Mummy looked drained but the adrenalin was keeping her going. She gave me and Nanna more gory details about the needles and thread they used over more strong cups of tea. It didn't seem much like the electronic game at all but if it all went well they might let him come home tomorrow or the next day.

"He will need physiotherapy and it will be a while before he can do stairs. He'll have to sleep on the sofa till he gets more mobile." Mum said.

"But what about when he wants to go to the toilet?" I had to ask.

"He will have to use a potty" Mummy said. Crikey, I thought, poor Michael.

"And how are you feeling Julie? This is all very upsetting. I've been praying for little Michael, praying for all of you." Nanna said earnestly.

"I will be fine once I know Michael is alright and he comes back home."

"And Brian?"

"No Gwen, no. I don't want Brian to come back home but I can't think about all of that until Michael is well."

"Oh. I see. I just thought maybe this might be one of those, those tragedy's that brings a family together. Consoling, bonding?"

"And who do you think is consoling him now Gwen, at work, after work?"

"Julie they have to work together."

"Do they? Did you know he had a car? Where did he get the money to buy a car?"

"I can't say Julie. Really I just don't know."

"Lies, deceit, drunkenness. That's Brian's code. It's how he lives his life Gwen. I am only now starting to see things clearly. Is that how you expect me and my kids to live, to continue to live? Ten bloody years of this I have had to put up with. Is this what I have to endure?"

"No Julie, of course not. Perhaps this is not the best time to talk about this." Nanna looked at me pointedly.

"No it's not. You're right" said Mum "But nothing's changed. Or perhaps I mean, he's not changed"

"It's affected him Julie, this terrible accident, you can see how worried he was about Michael."

"If you could stay until teatime Gwen I really would be very grateful. Then I will be home to look after Spangle. I don't know what I would do without your help."

"O Julie, this is heart breaking for all of us."

"I better get off or I'll miss the bus" Mum was tearing up as she kissed my forehead. "I love you Spangle!" she said. "You're a good girl. Perhaps I don't tell you enough"

"I'm sorry Mummy. I'm sorry about Michael. I was trying to look after him." She had made me feel overly emotional and all this just spilled out from nowhere. I wasn't quite crying but I was close.

"Spangle, don't for one minute think that this was your fault because it's not. It's really, really not."

"Off you go Julie or you will miss that bus. Spangle will be fine. I have bought some cross-stitch patterns we can do together."

"Thank you Gwen. Spangle, this is not your fault" She looked at us both a little sadly but then she dashed off. I felt relieved the awkward moment had passed but then I wished she was back and none of this had ever happened. Although I knew deep down it wasn't, it still felt a bit like it was my fault whatever Mummy might say.

Why was it always our family, why couldn't we be like a normal family, why does bad stuff always have to happen to us ? Why can't we be ordinary, normal, why not? Don't I pray enough? Aren't I good enough? Tell me, why us God?

CHAPTER TWENTY FIVE

Michael was home by the Wednesday, encamped, and resplendent in plaster of Paris and a beautiful new pair of paisley pyjamas, on the sofa. Mum had asked Uncle Ed to give her a lift to the hospital to bring him home. He was kind, reliable and happy to do it.

She had not asked Daddy to provide a lift even though she now knew he had means of transportation. I heard her telling Aunty Shirley the evening before that she had seen but not spoken to him at the hospital, when he had turned up to visit Michael with the new pyjamas as a gift. She said he had been very drunk and the nursing staff had refused to let him see Michael because he was 'using language' and waking up the patients. They had let him leave the pyjamas and then asked him to leave.

 I had not seen my Daddy since the night we spent together in the pub. I hadn't mentioned this outing to Mummy, she had enough other stuff to think about and I sensed she'd not be best pleased.

The nurses had given her special training on how to look after Michael at home. Medication needed to be administered, dressings changed, exercises done – it was never ending and there was no way Mummy could go back to doing her shifts at the chip shop at the moment. She said to Aunty Shirley that she didn't know how she was going to make ends meet but for now she needed to attend to her little boy.

"The children are my only priority." She said stubbing out her cigarette in a chunky cut glass ashtray.

Through this extraordinary summer Michael had experienced head injury, impalement, near drowning, and now a road accident. He currently sported a fracture with crutches, his left arm in a sling and a huge scab on his hairline on the side of his head. Nanna said, "You must be made of iron Michael, unbreakable!" though he looked as fragile as a bedraggled teddy bear. He was being feted like some kind of medical miracle boy. Seeing him on the sofa with the now familiar orange coloured Lucozade bottles close at hand I had never seen him look more content. He was the little prince of his domain. At least to begin with.

Nanna and Aunty Cathy both came to visit together that afternoon. The crutches upset Nanna because they reminded her of Grandad Harold's injury. He had old wooden crutches when he first came back from the war but didn't like using them.

"Will he have a limp Julie? Do they know if he will be affected by this when he's older?"

"They think the operation was a good set Gwen but they don't know for sure. The young ones usually heal well so please don't worry too much."

But Nanna did look very worried and she caught a sob in her throat. Aunty Cathy couldn't stay long as she had to get to the factory for her shift but she had bought us both a comic each and said she would see me at the gang show in a couple of days. She said that Nanna's minister was going to get us a special wheelchair with a raised bit at the front so Michael would hopefully be able to come too.

"Do you think Brian will…." Nanna began

"I can't think about him right now Gwen. Please. If you speak to him, could you ask him, could you tell him, that I need my housekeeping. That I have nothing. He needs to support his children. Whatever happens between us two he is still the father"

"Of course, Julie I will if I should see him. You know I am praying for you all."

"I know. Thank you." They hugged and then they broke away a little uneasily.

"It's a mess" Mummy said. "My parents will be here on Saturday and I have no idea what I am going to say to them."

"No."

"They never really took to Brian. They always thought he was a bad lot. My mother well, she's barely civil to him at the best of times. Perhaps I can keep it from them? But I can't just pretend everything is alright." She looked at Michael broken on the sofa.

"Perhaps.... perhaps everything will have sorted itself out by then?"

"I wish I could turn back the clocks. I somehow have to live with all this Gwen. But at the moment I have no idea how."

They both looked so glum. Michael was snivelling and fidgeting on the sofa. I went out to the kitchen to put the kettle on.

Please God, make everything turn out right. I said in my head. But God was working in mysterious ways and in the next few moments Michael let out a loud wail as he managed to stab himself in his injured leg with the knitting needle mummy had given him to relieve the itching.

"Ow oww!" he sobbed and then to everyone's amazement, "I want Daddy, I want my Daddy."

"Michael" snapped Mum. "Pull yourself together." Then she checked herself and knelt down gently before him. "Come on son, dry those tears, everything will be alright." She cradled his little blond head and it was clear that this recuperation was going to be a fraught one.

153

CHAPTER TWENTY SIX

After work the next evening Daddy did come home to visit Michael. He drove in his car with Aunty Rita in the passenger seat. They parked directly outside the front room window. I saw him peck her cheek as he left her there and he strode purposefully towards the garden path. There were a few kids playing football in the street and I could see them all watching him.

I went to let him in after glancing across at Aunty Rita observing her checking her own reflection in the sun visor mirror. She looked unruffled, calm and glamorous as ever.

Daddy came jauntily down the hall then into the front room. He was wearing his smart work suit. It was navy blue and he had a light blue shirt underneath it and a blue and grey tie. His after shave was very strong.

"Hello kids" he smiled as he gave us each a walnut whip which he took from his jacket pocket. The individual see through cellophane packaging made a crackling sound.

"That's from your Aunty Rita."

Michael sullenly put his straight down as Mummy turned and pointedly walked out of the room to set about noisily tidying up in the kitchen.

"Well then Sonny Jim" Dad said "and how are you feeling today? You don't half look as if you've been in the wars this time m'lad!"

Michael didn't reply.

"Crutches, scars and stitches. You'll look like Action Man by the time they've finished with you. Proper little solider"

Michael still made no response. He looked pale and tearful and he made a show of trying to look around Daddy to see the pictures on the telly.

"What you watching then?" Dad tried again.

"Anything good on?" Michael seemed not to hear him so he turned to me.

"And how are you Spangle?"

"Fine" I said quietly. I didn't know what to say.

"Well that's good then. I can't stop long. Julie." He stood up.

"There's a fiver on the mantle piece for you Julie girl. That's all I can spare. So don't bother asking for any more" He sneered towards the kitchen door and then continued, "Though I don't see why I should be paying anything when I can't even live in my own house. It's my wages pays the rent on this place you know that don't you? My hard work. My labour, whilst you sit around gossiping with the bloody nosey neighbours" His tone was getting a bit nastier. Mummy made no reply knowing better but still he continued, "Housekeeping! Not keeping house for me are you? Unless you think you can keep someone else's slippers warm. Is that what you think?" He was rambling horribly now.

"Do you Julie? Like that fat bastard from the chip shop."

"Don't be ridiculous." Mummy said from the relative safety of the next room but she knew it was best to keep quiet when he was like this. He stood up and started moving his arms around in his familiar angry way.

"My bloody house" he suddenly made a step towards the kitchen door, towards her.

"I don't know who the bloody hell you think you are! Telling me you want my money but I'm not good enough for you. What is

155

this? Women's bloody lib? Kicking a man out of his own home." He was getting himself more enraged when suddenly,

"Daddy, why do you like Aunty Rita more than you like us?" Michael spoke clearly and quietly for the first time.

Daddy was taken aback. He turned back to us. He hesitated and then tried to soften his voice,

"Michael, I don't know what you mean."

"Do you like her better than us?" No one spoke. I looked through the window at the older woman sat outside in what was obviously 'their car'.

"You must like her more if you go on holiday with her and you're always with her."

"I do like her Michael. Yes I do. I like her an awful lot. But I still like you." I could hear Mummy crying now.

"But you like her more." Daddy just stood there trying to think, to find the right words.

"Don't say that."

"Do you hit Aunty Rita?"

"No of course not. No. Never" Dad looked shocked, confused, flummoxed.

"But you hit us. You hit all of us."

"No Michael, no, only a smack if you are naughty. I don't hit you."

Then keeping his eyes on me and Michael, trying to read our little faces he reached into his inside jacket pocket taking out his leather wallet. I could see the satiny lining of his suit, the label of its maker, St.Michael, as he completed the deft movement whilst still looking at his children.

He coughed and then he pulled out another fiver and put it with the other one on the mantelpiece.

"It's not like that son. When you're an adult you'll understand." He reached towards him to try and ruffle his hair in his usual way. Though more or less paralysed by his accident Michael managed to pull away and a hurt look fleetingly crossed Dad's face. He looked out through the window to Aunty Rita in the car. He sighed then said,

"I'll pop round tomorrow after work to see how you are getting on?" He said in a tone that sounded like a question as he looked at each one of us awkwardly. Then with a bit more zest and confidence-

"Of course Dad the Bad likes you, Daddy loves you son. Daddy loves you all." But he sounded weary and a tad defeated. He stood up straight, smoothed down his jacket and then he was gone again. I watched him get into the driver seat of his car. He exchanged some words with Rita. She squeezed his arm and then put her head on his shoulder as they drove off slowly down Sycamore Drive.

Mummy came and sat down besides Michael and I came and sat on the other side of her. 'Dad's Army' was on and Michael smiled at something funny that one of the men had said. Mummy ruffled his hair as he gazed at the gogglebox.

"From the mouths of babes" she said and kissed his golden head. We all sat there for a few minutes watching Captain Mainwaring shouting at his soldiers.

CHAPTER TWENTY SEVEN

"Mummy please can I go out and play for a while? Tammy and Dawn are still out"

"Of course darling but only out the front where I can see you as it's starting to get a little darker now"

"We'll just practice our routines in the garden"

"Of course, good girl Spangle. I can't wait to see you in your performance. I know you will shine like a star!" She gave me a kiss and a cuddle.

I kissed her back and rushed upstairs to get my hard-soled shoes so we could practice the little bit of tap that I would do after my singing solo.

Just a few more days to go now, we were all very excited. Tammy and Dawn were pirates in another number and all three of us were fishes in the opening song. We had these parts nailed but my solo and the little dance I had to do needed work. We spread out along the garden path and started the song from the top. It was fun. We looked at each other and smiled as we enunciated our words and tried to make sure we hit the right notes- where bon bons play, on the sunny beach of peppermint bay! What magical lyrics for children to learn and sing. We loved this number. My singing solo halfway through was short but sweet and then I did a few quick step shuffles as Brown Owl had carefully taught me to do. Tammy and Dawn knew the steps off by heart too as we had gone over them so many times. We all laughed as we all made the same mistake in unison. Then we went straight back to the beginning and started again.

When we were tired and had gone over it enough times we lay down in the grass and looked up at the still blue sky. It was as blue as a sailor suit and a few evening stars were emerging and twinkling down on us in the distance far far away. Uncle

Ed had come round and cut our grass only that morning so the smell was heavenly too.

Dawn said her Mum had a new outfit to wear to the Gang Show on Sunday. Knowing Aunty Shirley it was bound to be eye catching. She thought there was a chance that a photographer from the local paper might be there so she wanted to look her best, just in case, Dawn told us.

I mentioned that my granny and grandad from the other side of the country were coming. But it had been a while since I had seen them and I couldn't properly remember what they looked like. I did know that they weren't as old as Nanna and they had a unusually big car. I think they both wore glasses too but that was about all I could really remember about them. O and red lipstick, my granny had trademark scarlet lipstick. They hadn't been to see us once in this house yet and the last time I must have seen them was during a long ago Christmastime when my Uncle Nigel and Aunty Nina still lived in this country, before they had emigrated to the other side of the world.

Tammy's brother Phillip was in the show too and so her parents would be in the audience. It was to be quite a turn out. The Chapel Hall would be packed to the rafters. Then Dawn asked me pointedly, curiously,

"Will your Dad be coming to watch you?" I hadn't thought about this. I felt alarmed.

"I don't know. I don't really want him to"

"Why not?"

"I just don't. Anyway I don't know if he is or if he isn't."

"My Daddy says he wouldn't miss it for the world."

"I think I'll go in now. It's getting late"

"Doesn't your Daddy live with you anymore?" Dawn persisted. She was her mother's daughter after all.

"Yes, no. I mean, I don't know."

"Does he live with that lady?"

"I don't know" I really did not want to talk about this. I felt unbearably uncomfortable. I was unbuckling my shoes ready to go in.

"Don't be mean Dawn" said Tammy "It's not Spangle's fault she lives in a broken home"

Dawn hadn't finished just yet.

"My Mummy says that Aunty Julie is going to be a one parent family."

"What's that?" I asked, not a little intrigued by all this unfamiliar lingo.

"O it's been on the telly and everything. It's the God's honest truth cos it's a documentary. Not acting. There's more of them every day. Mummy says there's one of them at Daddy's work. It's called a Single Parent. You get free school dinners if you become one of those."

"But I have packed lunch. I don't like school dinners. They make you have cabbage and custard and I don't like school dinners"

"Well I think if you are a one parent family you have to have free dinners. I think that's what they said on the programme"

"Well we are not a one parent family. I've got two parents, not one. They can't make me eat school dinners. I'm telling my Mummy." I said.

"They might not Dawn, you don't really know." Tammy interjected quickly seeing how upset I was getting.

"No they might not." said Dawn, it was clear she was pleased with her handiwork.

"I'm going in now." I said and pushed the door open, my dancing shoes in my hands.

"Goodnight Spangle" said Tammy in a kind voice, "see you in the morning. I think you did the dancing bit really well tonight". It was clear that dynamics were changing outside the house as well as inside and I felt very unsettled.

"Night Tammy." I raised a hand to both of them and Dawn flashed me a huge smile.

"Night, night Spangle." They both chimed in what sounded to me like a superior way.

Was this my own fault? If Daddy did leave us and go off with Aunty Rita it would be because I had asked God to make that happen. But would that mean I would have to eat school dinners and Mummy would become a single parent? O God I wish Daddy was just dead!! Wouldn't that be easier? Oh no, cancel that God. I didn't mean it. Just make everything turn out right, somehow, please God. Please make everything turn out right.

CHAPTER TWENTY EIGHT

Friday morning came after a fitful night of worrying and fretting about school dinners and the gang show and my grandparents coming to visit.

 Once more the sun blazed down on Little Loxwood and the rest of the country. I felt a sense of purpose as I was needed to go with Mummy to Fine Fare to get some nice food for when her parents, my granny and grandad arrived the following day. Aunty Beryl and Karen came to sit with Michael so Mummy and I could catch the bus to town centre. Aunty Beryl was helping him to do his hand and finger exercises.

"You're doing so well." she stated cheerfully. "Once your wrist is stronger we can have this sling off you and get you onto those crutches properly."

Michael was a little boy who desperately wanted to get moving and so he complied with whatever Aunty Beryl suggested. Plus, she had a plump white paper bag of flying saucers, his favourite sweets, on her lap as an additional motivator. This accident was in a different league to all his previous misfortunes. He looked forlorn and lost as we left him on the leatherette sofa.

The bus journey was only a short one. Down Oak Hill, our school on the right, past the parade of shops, then the fields and the swing park, cross over the bridge, onto the busy main road passing the biscuit factory and the railway sidings, then past the town's only tower block of flats, around the horse shoe shaped entrance to the precinct to be deposited in the concrete grey constructed bus station of the shopping centre. I knew this journey so very well and had even drawn a pictorial map of the route as part of a school project. Sometimes we walked in to town centre and got the bus back to save money, sometimes we walked there and back but today Mummy felt we couldn't leave Michael too long and she just wanted to get her shopping done as quickly as possible.

"Can we sit upstairs?" I asked.

"Of course we can." Mummy replied with a smile. I loved to sit upstairs, right at the front, if possible, so you could see in all directions and I could pretend in my mind that I was the driver. We navigated around the grassland where the swing park was all laid out tidily. I could see other children playing there. They looked a bit older than us and they were swinging wildly from the monkey bars. I couldn't help but think of the day of Michaels' accident and how happy he had been then. Perhaps because of circumstances with my father or because he had had so many accidents this summer not so many people had come to the house with gifts and cards this time round. This had made being an invalid less enjoyable for Michael and the novelty was quickly wearing thin. He was already bored and low spirited less than a week in.

Through the bus window I saw the dirty dark green trains parked up in their sidings, someone had drawn large smiley faces in their dust. One of them was winking and it made me smile. This journey was becoming a treat as, after the bus had negotiated our towns only roundabout, I had a great eye level view through the windows of somebody's flat in the high rise. A brief glimpse into someone else's world, someone with tartan wallpaper and a ceremonial sword on their wall. What kind of life was this?

The bus stopped in it's bay right outside the entrance to Fine Fare. Most of the ladies on the bus seemed to be going in there that morning. Under the concrete awnings of the town centre precinct it was fluorescently cool in its manmade shade, the orange logo a beacon to housewives.

I had my own special shopping basket which Mummy would put the lighter things in. She said we could have some tinned peaches and ideal milk as a treat and she was going to buy some tinned salmon and a cucumber to make a nice sandwich tea on Sunday after the show. She was going to buy some ingredients so that we could make a cake that afternoon as well. A Victoria Sandwich. My Mummy was exceptionally good at baking cakes. She was good at all cooking and she had won a prize for it when she was a schoolgirl. A National Prize. So it would be a nice tea once we had got all the things she needed.

Mummy had a list and we went carefully around the shop. She checked the prices of everything. I saw Stacey in there with her Mummy and we said a shy hello. They had one of those big trolleys, not a basket like us. Her cute little sister was in the seat thing at the front, smiling, gurgling and licking a swizzler lollipop. Her Mummy had her own car and they hadn't come on the bus like us.

Even though we had bought less than most of the other shoppers it seemed to have taken us a bit longer but soon we were back outside in the pedestrianised bus station waiting for the Little Loxwood Bus, the number 5. We moved towards our stand and as we did so Mummy stopped in front of an elderly gentleman. He had a walking stick and wore a straw sun hat and he seemed a little confused. It was very hot and dusty and the fumes from the bus engines thickened the air. There were a lot of bus stops close together and many people were milling about so I wasn't surprised when Mum took his elbow in a gesture of help. He looked shaky and glad of the support from a helpful stranger.

"Hello Tony" she said, "are you alright? You look a little bit hot and bothered. It's me, um Julie, do you remember?"

"Of course love. Yes. Of course I do. I am hot. Too hot. I need a seat and now I'm not sure if I need the 12 or the 12a. My route's been changed on the new timetable, but I'm not sure. Is this your little one?" He looked down at me. He had a short-sleeved shirt on and thick old mans' trousers. He was sweating profusely.

164

"This is my eldest Spangle. I think I mentioned her to you. My son is at home. He's er well incapacitated. I don't know if you heard? He had a road accident."

"I did hear and I was very sorry to hear it. Maybe you know already but they…your Brian and my wife are staying with my sister in law. And well she keeps me informed and I do talk to Rita a little so yes, very sorry. How is the little lad?"

"It's not easy for him being not able to move about but he's still with us which is a blessing in itself. It could have been very much worse" Mummy sighed. This must be Aunty Rita's husband! Gosh! I could not take my eyes off him. He was quite old and he did look a bit poorly. But he seemed nice and well, gentle. Almost like the total opposite of my Daddy in fact.

"Well it can't be easy for you either my love. Managing two youngsters on your own. Me I'll be fine when the temperature comes down a degree or two."

"I heard about your son." Mum said in a sad voice. "That can't have been easy."

 "No but I visited him only yesterday and they have got him on a car mechanics course in there and I'm still hoping he will come out better off than he went in. Might do him some good, you never know"

Mum smiled.

"And it seems I am about to become a Grandfather too so I consider myself to be a lucky bloke and I don't need anybody feeling sorry for me. You being such a lovely young woman with two beautiful children. I hope you feel the same." Tony gave my Mum a huge grin which she returned and said

"You know what Tony? I do feel the same. I am a very lucky person. It's good to have bumped into you and to be reminded of that." She beamed at him.

"Perhaps those less fortunate, unkinder people in our lives deserve each other." He wheezed and then half laughed, half coughed.

"You might be right about that. It is ridiculously hot. What do you say we go for a cold drink and Spangle perhaps you can have an ice cream?" I was taken aback by this extravagance but not about to decline.

"Best offer I've had in 'ears!" he said laughing and so we got ourselves un-entangled from the bus queues and made our way to the Wimpy opposite. All I could think of was the fact that Michael would die with jealousy that I was going into a Wimpy and that just made it all the more enjoyable.

Tony treated me to something called a knickerbocker glory. An entity hitherto unheard of and unexperienced but never forgotten. He bought Mummy a Coca Cola with ice and a slice of lemon and he had a cup of tea. Whilst we enjoyed these delights he gave Mummy a small white card which he said had the name and number of a good solicitor.

"Look out for your own interests Julie because no one else will. You are the injured party here." he said.

"I can't afford a solicitor Tony. I can't even pay the milkman."

"You are the injured party. You must stand up for yourself. You have rights you know."

"You don't know my Brian."

"I do, though not as well as you."

"Brian is not afraid of solicitors. He thinks the whole world revolves around him and that he can do as he pleases."

"If we let him think that, then he will. Are you strong enough to take him on Julie?"

"No" Mummy said meekly.

"No I'm not. I'm only strong enough to look after my kids"

"Talk to the solicitor. He can help. Just say that you will speak with him. Please Julie?" his voice was so gentle and coaxing.

"I can't see what good it would do Tony."

"What have you got to lose? Just make an appointment and tell him I recommended him. Please Julie. Those two will wipe the floor with you otherwise. They are two of a kind, especially when it comes to money. Vultures. Just go and speak to him. He's here in town. Helped me out many a time."

Mum did not look convinced.

"I don't even have his hourly rate Tony. I can't afford to speak to a solicitor. I have no real income and Brian knows that."

"Speak to him. Just call him on the phone. You need advice."

"You are a good man Tony. Thank you. I will give it consideration. My parents are coming tomorrow. God knows what they will make of all this. They haven't got a clue about what's been going on. The state of my so-called marriage. God knows what I will say to them."

"The truth. That's all you can say Julie. The truth. You have done nothing wrong."

"I can't see them seeing it like that."

There was a melancholy silence. I finished my ginormous ice cream slowly letting it melt down my spoon and licking it clean. We all walked back to the bus stops together, me carrying my little shopping basket on my arm proudly like Little Red Riding Hood. Mummy and Tony shuffling along more slowly having run out of things to say.

Mummy helped Tony to find the right bus back to Norton and then we got on ours. I pressed my face right up against the cool glass of the bus window and could not wait to get home to tell Michael and Dawn that I'd been to a Wimpy bar and had a knickerbocker glory!

CHAPTER TWENTY NINE

That afternoon the Minister appeared to descend on us as he came round to our house to visit Michael. The house smelt lovely because the sponges for the Victoria sandwich were just cooling on racks on the kitchen table when the front door knocked. Mummy answered and was both flustered and delighted by the sight of the bulky black wheelchair the minister from our Chapel had bought with him. He said we could borrow it for the gang show and as long as we needed it until Michael was able to get around on his crutches, which he said "Knowing Michael won't be all that long!"

"Can I push it?" I squealed with excitement. All the other kids were going to be so impressed with this.

"It's fantastic. Isn't it Michael? How kind of you to bring it round Reverend. Let's leave it under the porch for the moment. Though I don't know how we are going to manage going down the front steps by the gate." Mummy said pensively.

"We might need a big strong man to carry him it. O sorry Mrs Reid, I didn't mean… Of course I have heard about your family troubles."

"Perhaps Uncle Ed would help us or Des from next door" Mummy said.

Mummy helped Michael to come out on one of his crutches as far as the hall door so he could take a good look at it. It was square and large. He would be lost in its seat. It was made for a grown man but it was better than nothing. He did not look that enamoured with the old-fashioned looking contraption but he was interested in the prospect of a bit of freedom. The sofa was becoming his prison.

Mummy made the Minister some tea and I caught him eyeing up the cake but Mummy swiftly moved it into the larder out of his sight.

"Sorry I have nothing to offer you Reverend." she said "apart from tea."

"Most refreshing. I thank you. And how are things between yourselves? I mean between yourself and Mr Reid?"

"Mr Reid is not residing with us at present." Mummy said responding to his questions in the same language he was using himself and sounding somewhat stilted, odd and not at all like herself.

"Would you be expecting his imminent return?"

"I would not. I do not wish it."

"The family union is bless-ed."

"Not this one Reverend."

"Might I just say that the institution of marriage is sacred and of the highest sanctity Mrs Reid, dear lady? Divorce is final. It may be man's wish but it is not the Lord's wish."

"I have not instigated a divorce." Mummy said very quietly and sadly.

"Children belong in families. Forgiveness is Righteousness. Mrs Reid can I help you to find forgiveness in your heart?"

"I don't think you can. No"

"May God grant you the strength to live in harmony and acceptance and endurance with your husband."

"May God give me strength Reverend. It's not me you should be talking to. I find this conversation difficult."

"You are a faithful woman, bought up with a true faith. You bring your children to the Chapel. You worship the Lord Mrs Reid. God loves you"

"God has let us down Reverend."

"He has tested your faith. I can see that."

170

"My husband is an adulterer."

"That's an earthly sin."

"But it's a sin and it's not his only sin. He will not change. God cannot make him good or to act in a good way towards me and his children. God made him this way."

"We must love all of God's children. Even the sinners"

"And what about MY children? Must they continue to suffer at his hands too? No Reverend. I do not find forgiveness in my heart just as he has no repentance in his. I thank you for the loan of the wheelchair. I thank you for your advice. But I will not be heeding it. I do not wish my husband to return to us. I do not wish him for my husband"

The air was very still. Not one of us spoke as this absorbed into all of us from the air around us. I expected Michael to cry or say something but even he was still.

"I'm sad to hear you say that. I am." The Minister said morosely, shaking his head. "I'm very sad, I really am."

"Thank you for coming." Mummy was brusque with him now and clearly wanted him out.

"I will continue to pray for you all."

"Good day Reverend. Thank you again for the wheelchair. We will look after it and return it as soon as we can" she said almost slamming the door on his vampiric figure.

CHAPTER THIRTY

That evening Aunties Shirley, Doreen and Beryl descended as Michael and I were eating our supper of toast together on the sofa. After making quite a fuss of us both and getting a full update on Michaels injuries and his progress they swooped into the kitchen with German wine and cigarettes whilst Mummy put the telly on for us to watch. There was a trailer for The Generation Game which was coming back on in the autumn and then we were going to be allowed to watch "The Invisible Man".

Bruce made Anthea do a twirl which Aunty Shirley caught through the open kitchen door,

"O dear, apricot and avocado. Not sure even Anthea can pull that one off" she smirked. The cackling commenced and glasses were taken out of the cupboard as they settled themselves around the small table.

Mummy brushed her hand against Michael's forehead, but he tried to swerve past it to keep his eyes on the TV. He was excited about the programme. The ladies were going to help her carry him upstairs later so that he could sleep in his own bed tonight. He was so fed up of the sofa. Suddenly Mummy had an inspiration.

"Would you like to sit in Daddy's chair? We could put your leg up on the pouffe. You might find it more comfortable than lying on the sofa." His little face lit up.

"Really?"

"Well yes, you are the man of the house now Michael so I don't see why not." He beamed. Aunty Shirley came back into the living room and they both took an arm each and they helped him hobble the few feet across the room. I pushed Dad's pouffe closer to the chair so he could reach it properly and Mummy stuffed two cushions behind his back. He looked delighted and had managed the whole movement without once taking his eyes off the opening credits.

A few of Michaels friends had come round after the Minister had left partly to see the wheelchair better but also to keep him company for a while. They had drawn some funny faces on his leg with felt pen and written their names and he had seemed much happier afterwards. Now being allowed to sit on the special chair, to watch one of his favourite telly programmes was the icing on the cake. His diabolic injuries were finally starting to reap some dividends.

"Not sure Brian would be all that chuffed" Mum said to her friends as she went into the kitchen.

"But he's made his bed, so to speak" they all thought this was hilarious. I half listened to the telly and the aunties as the evening drew darker. I watched Michael's little face in the TVs glow. Would he really be the man of the house now? Daddy hadn't come round to see him today. Would he come tomorrow, would he come to the gang show? Was he dead because of my accidental prayer?

"I don't know what my parents will think" I heard Mummy saying. "They can be quick to judge."

"Well they can't judge you Julie."

"Well they will anyway. That's how they are. They will think it's my fault somehow."

"Julie you are their daughter. I am sure it will be nice for you to have them here. To talk to them, some comfort after all you have been through."

"You don't know them. But I have to face them. I can't change anything that's already happened. But I wish I could. I wish we could start all over again."

"O Julie. He would only do the same all over again. He's no good." Aunty Beryl spoke gently.

173

"And she's no good either, that Rita. They deserve each other, heartless creatures."

"She married that Tony for his money, divorcing him for every penny she can squeeze out of him even though she's the guilty party."

"Divorcing him?" Mummy said.

"Didn't you know? Well that's the rumour anyway."

"No I didn't know. I only saw Tony this morning. He never said. Though may be that's why he kept telling me to get a solicitor" Mummy paused and took a drag on her cigarette.

"She must want to remarry. She must be planning on marrying Brian." The shock and pain was tangible in Mummy's voice.

"They want to get married and to be together. So soon." Her voice trailed.

"We don't know that Julie. We are putting two and two together here and making five." Beryl said reasonably.

"They'll want this house. We'll have nowhere to live. They'll put us out." Mummy was crying now. "He's already said his name is on the tenancy and he won't give it up. What am I to do?"

"Now Julie, you really are jumping to conclusions. Even Brian is not that cruel."

"He is. He is"

"Julie love, have you got a solicitor?" said Aunty Beryl kindly. "Ours is very good."

"No why does everyone think I have the money for a solicitor?"

"Talk to your parents. They are sure to be able to help." My Mums sobbing increased.

"That bitch Rita better not think she can move in here. She won't enjoy a neighbourly welcome from me. Or from anyone else" Aunty Shirley stated emphatically.

"Don't even think it Julie. This is your home. Brian's hardly ever here anyway. They can afford their own place on the money they both earn. She's going to get a windfall from Tony too by the sounds of things." Aunty Shirley's confidence seemed to calm Mummy down a bit.

"Come on Julie love. Hey, hey, it might never happen and even if it does you're going to be fabulous in the role of beautiful divorcee. All the famous women are doing it these days. Look at Elizabeth Taylor. She's doing alright for herself. You just need to get Brian to give you a nice settlement." They all laughed at that. Then there was a silence as Mum looked at all her happily married friends and said from the heart,

"I never wanted to be divorced. I believe in marriage. I believed in my marriage, imperfect though it is. This is not what I want. I just want to be normal. A happily married wife. Married with kids."

They all went quiet. There was nothing anyone could say.

CHAPTER THIRTY ONE

The next morning was an absolute cleaning frenzy. My grandparents were due after lunch. They were not going to be sleeping with us, they planned to stay in a hotel in the town centre but they would be having tea at our house. On the Sunday they would be having lunch with us and of course, coming to the gang show.

Mummy was very snappy and clearly stressed so I used my initiative and cleaned my bedroom, Michaels bedroom and the bathroom as soon as I had finished my breakfast whilst Mum got on with the downstairs, cleaning and tidying around Michael. When I came down for the dustpan and brush she was cleaning the long narrow horizontal window in the hall that looked out onto the front of the street. I could see loads of my gang mates outside and longed to join them but knew what I had to do.

The smell of Windowlene was intoxicating and I enjoyed inhaling it as I swept down the stairs. By the time I reached the bottom Mummy had finished the windows and she got out the hoover to suck up the dust I had bought down and then she hoovered around the rest of the ground floor. I made Michael a drink of Nesquik and wiped down the surfaces in the kitchen whilst Mummy finished hoovering upstairs. The house looked very spick and span. No one could fault my mothers' domestic skills. She had cut some flowers from her border in the garden and put them on the sideboard in a striking green cut glass vase.

The kitchen was welcoming with fragrant herbs growing on the windowsill, the table laid with a crisp clean cloth and Mummy's well-presented homemade food on a chic, though brown, 70s tea set. The cake was filled and dusted with icing sugar and small fruit tarts and sausage rolls had also been made from scratch. She was going to do the tea and sandwiches fresh when they arrived.

I only hoped they would appreciate all the endeavour this had involved, Mummy's already broken heart was bursting with effort and anxiety.

I put the kettle on and made us both a cup of tea.

"Well there's nothing more I can do Spangle." And I had to agree, she had totally pushed the boat out. We sipped our tea side by side on the back step looking out at the houses at the bank. There was an ominous space to our left where Herbert used to be.

"I'll just give Michael a wash and a change of clothes and then they should be here within the hour."

"Can I wear my elephant dress?" I asked. This was my favourite summer dress that had been made for me by Nanna. It was a simple cut and beautifully sewn.

"You might be growing out of that now Spangle. You are getting so tall."

"Can I just try it on and see."

I did and it was too small for me but for some reason I was feeling stubborn and really wanted to wear it. Mummy looked at me with a wry smile as I stood in front of the mirror that had been screwed onto the inside door of my built in wardrobe.

"It's tight Spangle and it can't be that comfortable now can it?" she was right, it wasn't at all comfortable. But I did love it.

"Please Mummy. It can be the last time I wear it."

"If you really want to." she said as she brushed my hair.

"It is lovely material and those elephants are very sweet." She agreed as she deftly brushed the front tresses of hair nearest my face up into a ponytail leaving the rest to fall down over my back. The cotton fabric was a pale red and had tiny families of grey elephants marching from one side to the next holding onto each others' tails in a touching tableau of familial unity. She had a grey ribbon for my hair too which she pulled into a perfect bow around the ponytail.

Michael had on a smart white and blue cotton shirt and some pyjama trousers which were the only garments that we could get on him with his plaster. He looked a bit like a dishevelled aristocrat especially with his old brown teddy tucked under his arm. He resisted the wet flannel to his face to get rid of his Nesquik moustache but being immobile there was little he could do and Mummy also brushed his golden curls whilst she had him trapped.

I was positioned on the sofa to have a good view of our road and was inevitably the first to see the huge brown estate car roll up outside. My very tall grandfather emerged from the front seat. I was right he did have glasses and he was smartly dressed in a crisp short sleeved shirt with tie, topped with a light jacket. He walked around to the passenger side and opened the door for my grandmother and he stooped gracefully to offer her his arm. She barely looked at him and took his arm in a way that seemed as if she was hardly touching it. As I saw them through the window for the first time in at least two years I felt a wave of recognition and I remembered them as part of me, part of us.

My grandmother was a very striking woman both in looks and temperament. 1970s fashion trends had made no impact on her styling whatsoever. She wore a clingy 1950s style jersey dress in emerald green which embraced her curvy and attractive figure. A large bold silver brooch was pinned just above her heart. Her hair was in a Marilyn Monroe style though silver rather than blonde and she wore a court shoe on her stockinged feet. Her red lipstick and a trace of rouge completed the look. I immediately felt intimidated and it was with a nervous tremor in my voice that I called out, "They're here."

Mummy rushed over to the window, smoothed down her floaty summer dress and said, "Please go and let them in Spangle." I went down the hall to the front door and made it just before they had time to knock.

"Well hello there little Samantha" my Grandad beamed kindly "Not so little anymore. My you are growing up fast"

"Hello Samantha, can we come in?" Granny asked stepping into the hall in front of her husband. I widened the door so that he could follow. "Where's that naughty little brother of yours?" Mummy had written to tell them about Michaels' accident. "O dear Michael" she said when she set eyes on his small injured figure which was back on the sofa. "What have you been up to?"

"It wasn't his fault." Mummy said. "But it was very nasty and it's going to take a while before he gets back on his feet."

"I can see that Julie" her mother replied tartly.

"Now Vivienne, haven't we got some presents in the car for the grandchildren?" Grandad said already having to make the peace so soon into the visit.

"Go and fetch them please George." She commanded. "Julie, I am parched after that horrendous journey can you please put the kettle on without any further delay."

"Of course Mother" Mummy said and hurried out to the kitchen.

"And make sure you warm the pot before you fill it Julie. And sweetener for me please. I've given up sugar. Samantha dear, pass your Grandma that ashtray please."

My grandmother perched herself right on the very edge of Daddy's chair so she could lean towards the sofa and get a very good look at us. I stood next to Michael, not sure if anything else was to be expected of me.

"And where's your father Samantha? Down the pub I presume?"

"I, I don't…" I started to say just as Grandad came back with two nicely wrapped presents.

"Thank you George, make sure you give them the right ones". Mine was wrapped in flowery paper and Michaels was decorated in boats and from the shape they were both clearly books which is nice but is what they always gave us when they gave us presents.

"Thank you" we said in chorus as Mummy came out to have a look. She had put a pinny on and she was drying her hands in its skirt.

"Have you lost weight Julie? You look very gaunt. Is that husband of yours not feeding you?"

"I've prepared sandwiches and a light meal Mum. When would you like to eat? Now or …"

My grandmother broke her off, "I've not even had time to smoke a cigarette yet Julie and don't we need to wait for Brian to come home? Your father's not even sat down after all that driving."

"Well that's no problem, we can wait a while. I'll pour out the tea."

"It's probably stewed by now. If it is you had better make a fresh pot. Your father can't abide stewed tea and neither can I" I looked at my poor mothers frazzled face as she went back out to the kitchen. Michael and I had unwrapped our books and were looking at the illustrations. Mine was a book that teaches you how to identify flowers and I did really love it. So I kissed them both a thank you. Michaels was also a nature book about animals which was also just perfect for him and would give him something to look at as he whiled away his hours on the sofa.

Mummy came back in with two cups of tea on her best cup and saucers. Granny tapped out her first cigarette and immediately lit another leaving Mummy standing there with her teacup until she was ready to take it from her.

My grandfather was asking Michael about the accident and how he was feeling and Michael was glowing with the attention.

I noticed my grandmothers beautifully manicured and painted pointy fingernails. The shade matched her lipstick and her fingers were long and graceful, set off with elegant and rather large stoned rings. If you looked closely though the first two fingers were stained nicotine yellow.

I was still standing up and I must have looked awkward.

"Come and sit down on this pouffe near to me Samantha. Are you looking forward to the gang show? Do you know your part?" My grandmother was always asking questions without giving anyone the time to answer them but this time she looked at me and paused so I said, "Yes Granny."

"Now don't be nervous. I used to be on the stage myself so I know what I am talking about. Take my advice dear. Just block out everyone else in the room. Breathe slowly and be the part. I am sure you will be wonderful child."

"Yes Granny"

"Ugh I hate the word Granny I wish you could call me Viv or something, anything but that dreary old word. Makes me feel positively aged"

"Sorry Granny, I mean …" and unexpectedly she broke out into a huge and beautiful smile. She laughed. "You are funny Samantha" and gave me a peck on the top of my head.

"You can call me Spangle if you like."

"I wasn't sure if you had grown out of that nickname but I might just do that. Spangle. It does have a ring to it. Do you like your book? Perhaps we can make some sketches of some of those lovely wildflowers together later."

"Yes please" I said careful not to use the G word. I knew my grandmother was a very creative and artistic woman. She had her own studio in her home where she painted and she had been a head designer in a top advertising firm until she retired only recently. There was the stature of a 'boss' about her and Mummy had proudly told us how she had managed a large team of younger designers and was terribly well respected in her field.

"More tea please Julie" she commanded.

"Don't worry, I'll get it." I said taking her cup into the kitchen. Mummy was cutting the crusts off some sandwiches and arranging them nicely. I poured another cup from the pot and gave Mummy a smile before going back into the front room.

Grandad and Michael were laughing and chatting away.

"Would you like another cup Grandad?" I asked him. "Yes please little lady." He smiled. His was a gentler face. His thinning hair was grey rather than silver and his glasses were sturdy and horn rimmed. His face was manly and stubbly but had a softness to it and his eyes twinkled with love as he spoke with my little brother.

The room was warm and I opened a window before sitting back down with my grandmother. The atmosphere was tentative as Michael and I got to know our grandparents all over again.

"Spangle, I think you need to give me a tour of your house. I could do with a visit to the littlest room first though after all that tea." My grandmother said using a softer voice than the one she had entered the house with. I jumped up and took her by the hand. She slipped off her court shoes and let me lead her out to the hall and up the stairs. Whilst she used the toilet and washed her hands in the bathroom I checked that mine and Michaels rooms were perfectly tidy and opened the window in mine.

"What a colourful space!" she said, "you really do have the light in here. And look at these dear glass animals. Which is your favourite?" I told her I liked the bluey green turtle best and she agreed that he was very nice. I showed her the other bedrooms and although she didn't say much she nodded a lot.

Mummy and Daddy's room was very tidy and smelt of furniture polish. It faced the front of the house and had a huge window bordered with very flowery brown and peach curtains. Through it I could see the tops of the trees from the wood park behind the houses opposite. The sky was the brightest blue with not a cloud in it. I could see Granny was quietly noting every detail of the bedroom but it was spotless and tasteful and there can't have been much to find fault with. I looked outside and could see Uncle Ed taking something out of his car and felt the familiar pang of wishing he could be our father instead of Daddy.

Granny and I went back downstairs and in the living room Mummy and Grandad were either side of Michael helping him into the kitchen. They positioned him on his usual chair with a stool in front to support his plastered leg. Grandad ruffled his hair and checked he was comfortable before sitting down himself at the head of the table.

"We're not waiting for Brian then? I must say Julie the house is very pleasant. Better than the awful cesspit you used to reside in. If I had known how much better it was we may have visited sooner. Most light, clean and comfortable dear." The first kind thing she had said to her daughter since arriving.

"Thank you." Mummy responded. "We like it here. It's very friendly. The neighbours are nice."

"Do you see much of Gwen?" Granny asked pointedly.

"Most weeks, she's not that far away."

"Most weeks. I see." Granny took a sandwich. Grandad's plate was already filled.

"Really George. Anyone would think I starved you." He guffawed jovially as a response. Michael was filling his plate and his face too. Mummy had made a feast and it was delicious.

"Any Nig-Nogs?" Grandad said with his mouth full.

"What?" said Mummy.

"In the neighbourhood, any Nig-Nogs? Is it a good area?"

"Um only Carl from the barbers. A few in the factory I think. I don't know. Whatever does it matter Dad?" Mummy asked flustered.

He refilled his plate.

"I noticed a Chinese takeaway as we drove in but I suppose there's one of those in most towns nowadays." Grandad said.

"Well Carl's very nice. Kind to Michael when he cuts his hair. I don't know what you mean Dad. This is a very nice area. We like it here. More tea?"

"Your father's just showing concern Julie, there's no need to be rude. I'd like some tea please."

Granny reached down into the rigid leather handbag at her feet and pulled out an old-fashioned cigarette case. She had a ritual of tapping it then opening it. It was ornate black and white enamel and was a sophisticated looking trinket. She placed a cigarette in her mouth leaving a red smudge of lipstick on its tip and lit it with her gold lighter. Smoking at the

184

table was something neither Mummy or Daddy ever did. Mummy felt it was very rude to smoke whilst others were eating and even Daddy agreed with that. I could see Mummy wasn't happy but she didn't say anything. Granny barked at her husband,

"George fetch me an ashtray, what on earth do you expect me to do with this ash?" Without moving his body he reached out his arm and he slipped one deftly from the sideboard onto the table next to her tea cup. "You'll soon be on the mend Michael with an appetite like that. Most healthy." She continued blowing a plume of smoke towards him.

"Very nice spread Julie." Grandad said as Michael carried on putting as much food as he possibly could into his skinny little body. Mummy wasn't eating much. She smiled at Michael but she looked totally fraught.

I helped my mother clear away the plates. She sighed to herself as she went over to the sink to rinse them so that we could use them again for the cake. I took her perfect sponge sandwich from the pantry and placed it in the middle of the table to a gasp from Michael who due to his immobility hadn't seen the finished article. Mummy cut us all a piece each with an enamelled cake slice then she gave out matching pastry forks and we all tucked in. It melted in the mouth and was as light as air.

"Delicious" said Grandad.

"Bit tasteless" said Granny but ate it all anyway. As Mummy and I cleared away the table Grandad carried Michael back into the living room and made him comfortable on Daddy's chair. He took a deck of cards from his jacket pocket and started to show him some card tricks. I was looking through the door to get a look. "Go and see Spangle. I can clear up in here." Mummy said.

"No leave those Julie, come in here and sit down. Take the weight off your feet. You can do that later when we have gone." My grandmother had taken a little sketchbook from her handbag and was making a quick drawing of Michael which he hadn't noticed her doing. It was very good. He was smiling at Grandads tricks and jokes which were very entertaining. Grandad had a natural warmth and humour which Mummy must have inherited from him. He was very good with children and I wished Dawn and Tammy could see these tricks too.

"Come closer Spangle and get a better look." He said to me and as I approached Grandad reached his hand up behind my ear and pulled out a 10p. I laughed and then he pretended he was going to tickle me under my arms and pulled out 2 more, one from each armpit. He took out a huge white handkerchief with the initial G embroidered in it and made all the coins disappear right before our eyes.

"How do you do that Grandad?" I asked.

"Ah now that would be telling."

"Go on then tell."

"And get myself drummed out of the magic circle, no thank you." He laughed.

Whilst I was distracted Granny had drawn a sketch of me as well.

"You should draw something on Michael's plaster" I suggested.

"What a clever idea Spangle." She smiled and took some coloured drawing pens from a small leather pencil case within her handbag. She looked at me and smiled and said, "tell me when you know what it is" She sketched quickly with a black pen, shaded with a grey one and then added some background details in green and reds.

"They're my elephants!" I gasped. She had drawn a Mummy and two baby elephants, one bigger and one small walking in a line holding each others' tails like on my elephant dress. She was pleased I was so impressed and Michael flushed red with pleasure when he saw how good it was.

We all sat in the front room companionably. No one really saying much except Grandad as he teased me and Michael. Mummy was balanced at the very edge of her seat her hands clutching the skirt of her dress as her Mother chain smoked and sketched the room and threw out a few barbed words about dust on the light shade and the way the carpet was curling up under a piece of skirting in the corner.

"Brian needs to put a tack in that Julie. But he never was very handy around the house was he?" Mummy didn't react but just sat there clutching the skirt of her dress, like a child herself in this awkward situation.

"How about another pot of tea before your father and I need to go and book into our hotel?" Granny said to Mummy putting her sketch book to one side on the arm of the chair.

"Of course Mum." Mummy replied.

"I'll come and give you a hand." Granny said as she stood up and followed her daughter to the kitchen. "Now Julie. Where is this neglectful husband of yours?" she asked before firmly closing the door.

That door was closed a long time. Voices were muffled to begin with and then raised. Grandad looked up but didn't move from his post. He was reading us a passage from Michaels book and then asking us questions about animals we had seen on our visit to the zoo with Aunty Cathy. He was clearly trying to distract us but I could hear Mummy crying and I started to feel a wave of rising distress. I wanted to go to the door, I wanted to rush in and protect her somehow. I almost did but then the door suddenly opened and my grandmother strode out. Her face was furious as she bent down to pick up her handbag. She straightened her body to its full height and held the bag close to her and said sharply to her husband,

"Enough fun and games George. It's time we were off."

"O right dear, so soon?" he looked over her shoulder at my tearful mother in the kitchen doorway.

"Now. Right now. We will see you tomorrow children. Julie try to make sure my grandchildren are wearing clothes that actually fit them next time we see them. Spangle's dress is fit for a toddler." She strode to the door leading to the hall, "Come on George. I haven't got all day." Grandad was in the kitchen looking perplexed and trying to be kind to my mother who was drying her tears and saying, "I'm fine Daddy, it's alright, just go"

"Julie love, was it the nig nogs? Whatever is the matter?"

"George! Now!" my grandmother shouted.

"Viv really." He protested "whatever has gone on?"

My grandmother strode back into the living room with a dramatic flourish and held our attention as if she had just walked onto a theatre stage in a lead dramatic role.

"I'll tell you what's gone on. It seems YOUR daughter is unable to even keep a common shop boy happy George. A barrow boy from a prefab feels he can do better than your only daughter. Our child is not good enough! Julies husband has abandoned her for another woman."

"That's not quite what happened Daddy, I asked him to leave."

"Well bloody well ask him to come back then!" Granny screamed hysterically. My grandfathers face was ashen and confused. He put a tentative arm around Mummy's shoulders as she was properly crying hard now.

"There, there." He was saying as he patted her back. "There, there."

"No daughter of mine will be left high and dry and rejected by a working-class lout. Who the hell does he think he is? He's

188

got responsibilities. Good for nothing, he will never come to any good. I've always said so. Shameful that's what this is Julie. You have bought shame on this family. You have let some commoner from the gutter humiliate us" Granny was trying and failing to light a cigarette as she raged.

"Now Viv, please calm down. I am sure this can all be sorted out. Julie dear, Julie dear, please stop crying."

I could see Michael was ready to start crying. I felt numb. The room was silent for a moment. Then in a calmer, harder voice my grandmother turned to my Mummy and said nastily,

"Yes Julie, stop crying, stop bloody whimpering. Go out there and fix your wretched marriage. Do you know you look like a limp rag doll in that gypsy dress. So weak, just a door mat like that Gwen. No wonder you both get on so well"

Mummy collapsed on the sofa and I rushed straight over. I put my arm around her.

"Viv, it's time we went. You go and get into the car I will join you in a moment." Grandad tried to take charge. She looked at him head raised defiantly then exhaled a huge plume of smoke before doing as she was told and turning on her heels.

"Now Julie." Grandad said firmly but gently. "Pull yourself together and we will talk about this when your mother has had time to calm down. She's just upset and worried about you all. I will come round later when the children are asleep to try and get a clearer picture." He got himself a cigarette from the pack he carried in his jacket pocket and then he also lit another and passed it to my mother.

"It's not my fault Daddy" she said in a whisper.

"Every problem has a solution." He said kindly before leaving us to go out to his car and face his angry wife.

CHAPTER THIRTY TWO

Later I heard Grandad come back that evening as I lay in bed. To begin with there were more angry words this time between him and my mother as he struggled to understand his daughter as she tried to unravel the last ten years of her life with some shred of dignity. This time she didn't cry though and the voices eventually calmed to a more level tone. He was there for quite some time as I must have drifted in and out of sleep. I heard an owl toot once or twice and a squally cat fight in the distance. A few phrases drifted upstairs to my little room but their conversation was mostly private, as it should be, between father and daughter.

As she walked my Grandad down the hall to the front door to say goodnight I heard Mummy clearly and calmly say, "I can't take him back Dad. Not after what he's done this time. I just can't. I won't. Tell Mum don't try and make me." Grandad sighed then said,

"Your mother can't stomach a divorce, she's worried about the stigma. Those other women in the Siroptomists, her so called friends, she feels, well she… Well let's not worry about that now, she's in shock. You look pale, you must be exhausted. Get some sleep Julie. Have an early night. Your mother says not to bother making Sunday lunch for us. We will eat in the hotel instead and will meet you at the Chapel for the gang show afterwards. Less work for you eh?"

"Daddy please don't let her make me take him back. He's….."

"I'd like to get my hands on him. I really would Julie. Get some sleep dear. We will see you tomorrow." It sounded like he gave her a quick kiss goodnight before leaving and driving off in the battered old estate car.

I heard Mummy bolt the front door after him and then go to the kitchen and do the same there before filling up the kettle and putting it onto boil. I could hear her moving around quietly. Before she had time to drink her tea there was a loud bang at the front door. Not a knock on the knocker but a thud.

My radar was activated and I slipped out of bed to sit on the top step of the staircase. Someone outside opened the letterbox, they must have been looking through it. Then it snapped shut and they rattled it loudly. I heard my Daddy calling.

"Julie, Julie. Let me in love. I've come home to you. I've come back. The wanderer returns. Let me in love, let me in my own home." His voice slurred but it was not raised. He was trying to sound kind. "I've missed you love. It's time for Romeo to come home to his Juliette. Let me in now love."

Mummy made no reply or movement.

"Come on Julie. What you gonna say to Viv and George? They must be wondering what's going on. Lover's tiff and all that. Come on love. Time to kiss and make up eh?"

No reply or movement. Dad went quiet too, clearly having a think about his strategy.

"Julie? Julie!" his voice getting a bit louder now. He banged again but this time really hard on the door with his fists. Through the long narrow hall window below I could see the lights go on in Uncle Ed and Aunty Beryl's house opposite.

Daddy banged the door again.

"Let me in you bloody bitch. Open up! Let your awfully wedded husband into his own home." He laughed at his own joke.

Again Mummy did not react or move. He gave the door one final thump and then I saw his shadowy form scuttle off down the path. Uncle Ed opened his front door and gave him a disgusted look but said nothing. I sneaked down a few more stairs so I would have a better view and I saw him open the door of his little green car and get in. He was smirking to

192

himself in the greenish interior car light. He puffed out his cheeks and then blew out as he turned the ignition and slowly pulled away.

I hadn't heard her coming and when Mummy suddenly opened the front room door and came out into the hall we both gave a startled jump as we saw each other.

"O Spangle!" she said perturbed and then with a gentle smile "Right young lady, up to bed with you pronto. Big performance tomorrow. It looks like it's going to be a big day for all of us. Up you go!" I leaned forward to kiss her and then did as I was told. I said my prayers again and wondered what kind of day it would be and how it could possibly be even bigger than this one.

PART THREE

Dancing Queen

"Dancing Queen, feel the beat from the tambourine

You can dance, you can jive, having the time of your life

See that girl, watch that scene, digging the Dancing Queen"

CHAPTER THIRTY THREE

It was the last weekend in August, the Bank Holiday and you could taste in the air that the summer was coming to its close. There was a faint sniff of mould and leaves were already starting to turn to their rust colours on the trees.

But that Sunday morning was still another gloriously sunny and warm one when I opened my brightly patterned bedroom curtains to assess the world. There was a knot of nervous apprehension in my tummy as I looked over to the houses behind ours. Their curtains were open but it was a bright morning and I could not see into their lives.

I looked at their gardens which were scorched and hard from the long drought. Their lawns were just tufts of straw on cracked grey soil. Ours had faired a bit better because Uncle Ed had been cutting it regularly when he did his and we had been watering it each time we had emptied the paddling pool. It wasn't lush but it was greener than most. I breathed in the morning deeply. There was a whiff of dampness in the atmosphere and a couple of clouds hung in the sky but it was a beautiful start to the day.

Michael was up and out on the landing in his pyjamas grappling with his crutches. He was getting the hang of these fast and he got into a rhythm as he moved forward toward me. He heaved a little in his breathing but it didn't take long before he independently got to the top of the stairs for the very first time. He passed his clumsy wooden crutches over to me then carefully put out a hand to each wall to take his weight as he slid himself down to a seated position on the top step. His broken leg shot out horizontally in front of him over the first stair. It looked quite small and the colourful scrawls accentuated its childishness. Michael took a deep breath in and then he turned back to me and gave me a cheeky smile.

Without saying anything he bounced slowly down from the top, stair by stair on his bottom laughing and giggling as he went.

"Mummy, Mummy." he called out on reaching the final step and landing in the hall and our mother came running from the kitchen to see what was going on. "I did it on my own" he said as he smiled at her, "All by myself!"

"I can see. Well done my darling." She kissed the top of his golden head. Her cheeks were flushed with her love for him. "Now let's get you into the kitchen and make you comfortable. Rice Crispies or Weetabix?"

I was too excited to eat but Mummy made me have some toast and tea. Nanna was coming over on the bus soon to help. Whilst we ate our breakfast at the table Mummy was outside the backdoor with a bowl of warm soapy water sponging down the ancient black wheelchair, which was to be Michaels chariot to the gang show. She put it in the middle of the back path in the full sunshine to dry and she had some comfy cushions ready to put on it so that Michael could be boosted up and would be able to see the show properly.

Aunty Shirley called across to Mummy from over her fence two doors down.

"Dawn says would Samantha like to come round for a last minute practice?" she asked.

"Yes please Mummy, can I?" I said leaping down from the table and into the garden.

"Just for an hour then please Spangle because by then Nanna will be here and we will have to start ragging your hair." I bolted upstairs to get washed and dressed and was round at Dawns in no time. We pushed back the furniture to the edges of her front room to make a stage. She seemed just as nervous as me and we only practised the songs once as we didn't want to jinx it. We were sprawled on the sofa talking about whether we thought anyone would make any mistakes and if everyone would turn up. Dawn liked an older boy in the scouts and she was anxious about making a fool of herself in front of him. She talked about him incessantly. He was going to be holding and swaying a flag in one of the numbers and she was to be stood right in front of him, inches away from his arm. She was thrilled almost to the point of nausea by this.

Dawn was going to be wearing her wavy brown hair up and her Mummy had her costumes laid out on the ironing board in their kitchen. She was starching them to within an inch of their lives and it made a nice clean linen smell in their house. We were so excited we could hardly speak or play or concentrate on anything and we were now just idling and watching the minutes tick away on the carriage clock which sat on their faux marble mantlepiece.

Dawn's Daddy, Uncle Sandy was polishing her black dancing shoes on their back step. He was brushing away and whistling to himself as he placed one completed small shiny shoe on the newspaper he had put down to catch any dirt or polish flecks. This added a new intoxicating fragrance to the mix in Dawns house. I had better go and clean mine, I thought suddenly and jumped up from their beige leatherette sofa.

"Call for me on your way up!" I called to Dawn as I made my way out their front door.

I flew up the garden path and in our back door. Nanna was there in the kitchen already putting on her pinny. Her wicker basket full of strips of old sheets was parked on the kitchen table ready for rolling. She turned the radio dial until she found some hymns on the radio and then Nanna pushed a kitchen chair as close to the sink as she could get it. I jumped on and hung my head over the basin. Nanna put an old towel around my shoulders. She had a plastic measuring jug which she was partially filling from both the taps until she got the correct temperature. Then she soaked my hair thoroughly, shampooed it and soaked it again. Then came the very worst bit which was combing it all through with a wide toothed comb.

197

She tried to be gentle but my eyes were watering by the time she was finished.

Nanna was singing along to the hymns as she vigorously detangled my locks. Then as I sat on the same chair she worked in some very pungent smelling setting lotion and got to work, a tress at a time, rolling my hair up tightly in the cotton strips. When they were tightly rolled she knotted them up and and then stabbed them with hair grips into my skull. It took ages and it hurt from time to time as she pulled, tugged and twisted my hair. But I didn't complain. I looked up at the picture in front of me on the kitchen wall opposite. It was of part of a walled garden, a herb garden because the plants all had their names next to them on wooden pegs. I imagined I was very, very small and that I was walking around underneath the foliage, cool and sheltered where no body could see me. I could smell the damp earth and the fragrance of thyme and sage as a crackly congregation sang thanks and praise for all God's gifts around us, as sent from heaven above.

"Right now stop your day dreaming Spangle and go and fetch me your dresses and your hair ribbons so I can give them all a quick press with the iron please." I suddenly heard Nanna saying. "and ask your mother to bring down the hair dryer when she has finished dressing Michael."

"Yes Nanna and I will clean my own shoes. I know how to do it because I did it for one of my Brownie badges." I said scooting off upstairs with a head full of knotted hair and bedsheets. The house was a hive of activity. Mummy was combing Michaels hair and getting ready to help him downstairs, not that he needed it. She had bought a chicken that she had planned for her own parents and had decided that we would all enjoy it anyway so she set about dressing it for the oven as I sat on the step and shone up my dancing shoes. I was determined to do an even better job than Uncle Sandy had done with Dawns.

Nanna looked down at me and shook her head in a sad and resigned manner and said, "Your father should be doing that." But I said nothing. She unfastened her floral pinny and gave it a good shake out into the garden before putting it back on again then she went in to help Mummy with the veg.

"We don't need Brian, Gwen. We can manage very well on our own. Just as you managed without your Harold." I heard Mummy say to her calmly.

"I don't want to fall out with you Julie. Especially not today."

"Good, could you pass me that stuffing and do me a few more parsnips? I am grateful for your help."

"There's not a day goes by that I don't miss my Harold."

"Of course." They looked at each other solemnly.

"Do you think he'll be coming today to the chapel to watch Spangle? Brian I mean, Harold is always with us all."

"He doesn't keep me informed of his plans. I doubt if he even remembers that the show is on, let alone on which day."

"Tut!"

I bought my shoes in and put them under the coat stand in the hall then went to join Michael in the front room. He was doing some colouring and had his golden head down in his lap where the book sat on a dinner tray. He was separate from us, in full concentration. In his Michael world.

I didn't know what to do with myself. Time was going so slowly and I wouldn't even be allowed to put my costume on until after the rags were taken out and that would be after dinner which would be ages.

"So Viv and George won't be joining us for lunch?" Nanna asked even though Mummy had already told her that. This day was overlong already and we hadn't even got to lunchtime.

The hymns had finished and the news came on so Mummy switched the radio off.

"You'll see them at the Chapel." Mummy replied. "It's easier if they go straight there."

"How is your Mother?" Nanna asked cautiously.

"No change." said Mum opening the oven door to check all was OK with the meat. The potatoes in the saucepan on the hob were bubbling so she drained them off and placed them around the chicken in the roasting pan. She added some salt and put it all back in the oven. "Same as ever."

"O" said Nanna. "Can I do anything to help?"

"You go and keep Spangle company, she looks nervous and I will make us all a cup of tea."

"I don't look nervous." I called out.

"Big ears!" called back Mummy laughing.

"She looks funny though with those things on her head" said Michael.

"Not as funny as you with that thing on your leg." I retorted.

"Now children" said Nanna, "No need to be cheeky on the Sabbath."

"What days can we be cheeky on?" Michael asked cheekily.

"Well I can see you're on the mend." Nanna replied to him. "How about a nice Sunday story whilst dinner finishes cooking?"

"Only if it's Noah's Ark." said Michael and so she sat down and told him the long boring story of Noah's Ark whilst I mooched around moving from sofa to windowsill, half listening and half gazing out the window. Mummy bought us cups of tea and then aimed the hair dryer at my head for a while so that the lotion could set my hair in the required ringlets.

200

Then I helped Mummy lay the table and before long we were eating dinner. I had thought I wasn't hungry but the chicken was tasty. I wolfed it down with plenty of roasties and gravy and so did Michael. Then Mummy parked Michael on the sofa with some of his army men to keep him occupied. Nanna stayed in the kitchen and did the washing up whilst Mummy took me upstairs to put my first outfit on and to get me ready- at last!

My first costume was a pretty very bright yellow dress with puffy sleeves. It was for a number about the sun having his hat on and some of us girls were little rays of sunshine. Mummy had bought this dress from her catalogue and apart from trying it on this was the first time I had ever worn it. Neither Tammy nor Dawn had seen it either.

The second outfit, the lovely little sailor girl dress, that Nanna had made me was ironed and hanging on a small coat-hanger which Mummy covered with a see through plastic bag ready for her to take up to the Chapel to give to Brown Owl for my later 'Star' number.

Mummy sat me on the stool in front of her dressing table in front of her huge mirror. There was a big one in the middle and two moveable wings on either side of it which could be positioned so that the sitter could see their head, face and hair from every angle. She had a pointy tight toothed combe and she used the sharp handle to help her undo the tight knots of sheet and to unravel and take the rags out of my hair. Sitting there I couldn't help but admire the yellow summer dress, it was just a perfect buttercup yellow with white brodcrie anglais around the neck and sleeve hems. It was a shame the summer was almost over as I doubted I would have many more chances to wear it. We would be back to school on Wednesday, perhaps Mummy would let me wear it to school.

My hair was falling onto my shoulders with a bounce. Each ringlet was tight and springy and the whole effect couldn't have turned out better. I shook my head when Mummy told me to and she pinned a few coils higher around my face and tied them with white ribbons. Then she told me to close my eyes whilst she sprayed on some hair lacquer. The smell was intense but gosh I felt so grown up.

Mummy put some elastics around the top of each of my white socks and then folded them back half an inch to cover them. Then she put my shoes on, "Very well polished she said." Smiling. "I am very proud of you Spangle, you look fabulous. Much prettier than Shirley Temple."

"Whoever she is." I said happily. My Mum gave me a kiss and a cuddle and then she followed me downstairs carrying the sailor dress. As we got down into the hallway the front door knocked and Tammy and Dawn were both stood there waiting for me in their own yellow dresses, both quite different from mine, thankfully.

"Right off you Dancing Queens go then." Mummy said. "I will be up shortly and will come backstage to do your make up and bring in your sailor dress and Brownie Uniform. Don't get dirty or scuff those shoes on the way up there, mind you Spangle. And remember to listen carefully to everything that Brown Owl says. Good luck girls!"

"Love you Mummy, see you in a little while." I said giving her a kiss goodbye.

"We are the dancing queens today aren't we?" said Dawn. "We must listen to the Top Forty when we get back and see if that's gone to Number One or not."

And off we went on the ten minute walk up to the chapel singing Dancing Queen all the way in the last of the August summer sunshine. "OOOOOooo ooo oooo   see that girl, watch that scene, dig it the dancing queen."

CHAPTER THIRTY FOUR

Back stage in the hall of our chapel was a throng of chatty excited children. The Brownies were stage left with some Girl Guides and the Cubs and Scouts were stage right. Brown Owl and Tawny Owl's uniforms were crisply ironed and absolutely immaculate. But at least they looked friendly. The taut uniformed men that were in charge of the cubs and scouts looked terrifying and seemed ready to send their little charges off to the front line of battle.

I don't know about the boy's side but the girls had wooden benches to sit on under our own named coat pegs and a long table had been placed in front with a few stand up shaving mirrors, boxes of stage make-up and hair brushes interspersed along their length. There was also a full-length mirror by the door leading to the curtain onto the stage so you could have a last full frontal glimpse of yourself before facing your audience.

Tammy, Dawn and I could not resist slipping through the black painted door for a quick peek through the curtains. We giggled at our yellow selves in the mirror on the way through and then we were scrabbling with the heavy, dusty blackout curtain to get a glimpse of the hall. Empty and set up as a theatre auditorium it looked huge and so different from when it was our Brownie meeting room.

Directly below the stage, in a semi-circle, were chairs facing metal music stands already set out with sheet music. There was also a small podium, presumably for the conductor. A jet black upright and aged piano sat to the right of this set up with its own special light pointed at the music rest. Facing this home-made orchestra pit and the stage were many rows of metal framed stacking chairs with wooden seats and backs.

This space was where us Brownies normally ran around and played indoor team games with bean bags, balloons and hoops. It suddenly looked bigger, more formal and well, serious.

The high windows on either side of the hall had their thick black curtains drawn down to completely cover them and block out the natural light and the minister and the chapel vergers were opening the fire doors to let some fresh air into the musty cavernous space.

Through the obscured glass doors on the other side of the hall that led into the ante room sounds and shapes of people, our loved ones, filtered through.

I felt butterflies flitter in my tummy.

"How many people do you think will be coming?" I whispered. I could hear Tammy trying to count the seats.

"Fifteen either side, that makes thirty each row. Twenty two rows, or is it more, I might have lost count, that makes um ….."

"It's an awful lot anyway." said Dawn. "I can't wait to see my Mummy and Daddy I but wish my silly brother wasn't coming. Andrew's just so embarrassing. He laughs in all the wrong places and can be so very silly"

"My gosh I think it's more than 600 people." I exclaimed in my quietest voice. The enormity suddenly dawned on me.

"No Spangle, surely it can't be that many?"

"It might be more." I replied quietly mortified. Everyone from Sunday School, Chapel, most of our neighbours, my immediate family and lots of people from school and all their parents were about to watch us prancing about being rays of sunshine and watch me pretend to be a Hollywood child star I had never even seen a photo of let alone seen performing the number we were planning to do. And the huge finale at the end with all of us in our uniforms - what if I forgot my words or the routine or my steps? This could easily be the very worst day of my life so far.

"We better go backstage." I sighed and we draped the curtain back to how it was and slipped back through the inky door into the light drenched dressing room.

The three of us were humbled and less chatty now and sat down in our spaces. Tammy's Mummy came in and put some lipstick on her and dusted her face with powder. She left us a packet of fizzy orangeade Spangles to share, making a kind joke about my name. Then my Mummy and Aunty Shirley came in together. Dawns face was given a full and careful make over as Aunty Shirley took full control of the make-up box. Dawn looked like a porcelain dolly on a shelf by the time Aunty Shirley was finished. I hardly recognised the features that I saw every day and knew so well.

Mummy twisted a few of my curls around her fingers and sprayed them with more hair lacquer. She put a dab of rouge on each of my cheeks and then swept over it with a soft brush and some light powder and that was it. I was ready for my moment in the spotlight.

Mummy leant towards my ear so no one else could hear and quietly told me that I was the warmest, brightest ray of sunshine in the world and all I needed to do was to go out there and shine. I looked up at her pretty, young face and took strength from her encouragement and kindness. She gave me a kiss and then she stood up and said,

"Come on Shirl, there's nothing more we can do here now, it's all up to our girls now to do us proud!"

"Give them the old razzle dazzle!" Aunty Shirley said throwing an exaggerated cheeky wink in our direction before stretching out, unfolding her long gangly body and slipping away with my Mummy back into the auditorium.

We all looked at each other and smiled as Tawny Owl came in and said in clear, firm tones

"Six minutes to curtain, girls. Six minutes."

CHAPTER THIRTY FIVE

Before we had time to think, blue clad Guides filed in and stood before us in rows. Brown Owl told us that when she raised her hand we must follow them onto the stage but to remain silent. If we spoke the hall would hear us and we would ruin the Ministers speech to the congregation as he officially opened the Gang Show. Dawn and I looked at each other. I knew I, for one did not want to ruin anything.

Us Brownies looked so little next to the Guides who seemed tall, sophisticated and self- assured. Some of them were wearing eye make-up! They looked a bit confident and jaunty like the St Trinians girls and I couldn't wait to one day be one of them.

We silently followed the Guides, filed in and stood in front of the beautifully painted stage set of a rural landscape with a huge smiley sunshine face dominating the skyline.

It was dark and very, very hot. Hotter than July. No air. Someone behind us fainted loudly and a Guide took her out as the rest of us stood quiet and dizzy as the Minister came onto the stage to polite applause.

"Ladies and Gentlemen. I would like to welcome you to God's House, our very special Methodist Chapel here in Little Loxwood. You are all more than welcome and it is very humbling to see such a large congregation here in our community hall this afternoon."

Polite applause.

"Our local young people have worked so hard to put on a wonderful show as the climax to what has turned out to be an astonishing and memorable summer. We thank God for blessing us with his warmth and radiant sunshine these past few months. Today I sincerely hope that you will all have an enjoyable, indeed fun-packed afternoon. Soft drinks and ice pops are on sale in the ante room and teas and coffees can be purchased from the kitchenette during the interval and at the end of the show. All the proceeds will go to the Senior Citizens Christmas Party. Thank you all so much for coming along to support the Brownies, the Cubs and the older children in their endeavours."

Slightly louder applause.

"And now, without further ado, to open this magnificent event I would like to introduce the Mayor of Loxwood, the honourable Clement Morgan!"

What???? The Mayor? How long was this introduction going to take? Kids were melting behind this haberdashery!

"Ahem, Ahem, thank you, thank you all very much. Too kind, too kind." Someone old and crotchety sounding coughed out to the audience of bored family members who wanted to see their children sing and dance.

"So ahem. Thanking the Minister here and the Scouting movement and Baden-Powell and all that. I er officially declare the Summer Gang show of 1976 open and er ready to entertain you!"

"So in that case, take it away young people." said the Minister as the band started up its refrain at long last and the curtain lazily dragged itself back from the centre to the sides of the stage.

CHAPTER THIRTY FIVE

We came on quietly and took our positions as the refrain from the piano gained momentum. I was prepared for the blinding glare of the stage lights from our rehearsals and as my eyesight slowly settled down I started to scan the seats in my line of vision for sight of Mummy and Michael. Because of Michael's wheelchair I found them quickly. They were right at the front on the end of the row at the right-hand side. Mummy was in the last seat to be next to his chair and they felt very close to the stage. I felt so high up looking down on them. Behind Mummy's head I could see Aunty Cathy and Nanna and next to Nanna were Granny and Grandad. They were all in their Sunday best with Granny Viv in a glamorous dress suit with a feathery thing in her hair dramatically arranged to sweep across her forehead.

Nanna had a nice floral dress on, a bit old fashioned but with a smart jacket on top. She had a small hat on top of what looked like a new wig. Aunty Cathy looked very pretty in a fashionable floaty dress with smocking on the front and the sleeves. Aunty Shirley had also managed to get into the front row and was sat next to Mummy but Uncle Sandy and Andrew were further back. As we started to sing the first notes of our opening number my eyes flitted around as many of the other seats as I could manage and I picked out Aunty Doreen with Karen and Uncle Tom, Tammy's Mummy and Daddy and her little sister. Aunty Sheila, Aunty Beryl and a lady from the flats were together near the middle of the audience and I could see two ladies from the sweet shop and some teachers from school back toward the last bit of the hall that reached the light. Then I decided to stop looking and concentrated on the words and our movements around the stage and before I knew it the first number was over and we were bowing to rapturous applause.

As I raised myself back up I only had eyes for Mummy who was looking straight at me, clapping and smiling. I smiled back at her with happiness and relaxed a little and started to enjoy myself.

The Sun has Got His Hat On almost tore the roof off the chapel the amount of cheers and applause we all got. It was dizzying. Intoxicating.

Next up some Guides and Scouts did a sketch set on a desert island involving a stuffed parrot and some buried treasure. I didn't really get the joke but it looked very colourful and the audience were in uproar.

A tiny Cub in a miniature navy uniform played a mournful and moving trumpet solo and two younger Brownies dressed as chaste looking mermaids sang a duet of an ancient folktale whilst perched on a fake rock draped with seaweed.

I did catch Michael laughing at a few of the skits especially one of the routines the Cubs put on. Two of them pretended to be Laurel and Hardy moving a ladder around the stage with an open pot of paint on the top rung. They were meant to be getting a boat ship shape and some of us Brownies were background people and had to stand on stage and gasp appropriately. I could see Michael clearly and he was in hysterics at this, tears of laughter glistening down his cheeks. It warmed me to see him enjoying himself and I knew Grandad would be loving this too.

I needed to get backstage now to change into my sailor dress. Brown Owl helped me and then put a bit more rouge on my cheeks before handing me my prop, a huge spiral pink and yellow cardboard lolly.

Some Cubs and Scouts dressed as sailors and pirates were onstage and we could hear them belting out a raucous sea shanty. They were stomping and swilling ale and slapping their thighs and the audience were clearly lapping it up.

But then, all too soon, it was time for my big number- The Good Ship Lollipop. My tummy was in knots as Brown Owl propelled me back towards the black door and then lined up a little troop of girls behind me. The Pirates and Sailors remained on stage as backing singers and dancers too and suddenly, as the applause died down, Brown Owl gave me a firm push through the door towards the side curtain and there I was on the wooden treads of the stage in the glare of an intense spotlight. The room and stage were silent.

The rest of the stage and the audience were in darkness. Pitch darkness. I froze for a moment. Then I heard the little band start up the familiar introduction to the song I had practised hundreds of times. The melody I knew inside out and back to front. I took a deep breath and raised my curl filled head to face a vague spot somewhere in the middle of the huge room.

The pianist and the little orchestra were positioned directly in front of me but I heard the music only in the distance as the swooshing noise that my blood was making in my ears as it pumped around my body was unusually loud. But my mouth was open and I must have been singing because I became aware that I could vaguely hear that in the distance as well.

Although I was aware that I was moving around the stage and my hands were making practised actions I felt as if I had no control over anything that any of my body parts was doing.

The music lulled in the middle of the song, then repeated and I shuffled to stage left and started my little tap dance. I paused and the brownies behind me were illuminated and then they copied the exact same steps I had just done. Then the spotlight was back on me as I did the next little shuffle, gave a cute smile, took a pretend lick of my lollipop and then burst back into song. I repeated the chorus, sang the refrain with all my heart and soul and then bowed as the lights went off. I just had time to take a deep breath before the lights came back on and lit up the whole stage. I stood up, almost floored by the wave of noise that came towards me from the audience. I could feel that my cheeks were aflame with a hot blush. I could also feel little dribbles of salty water trailing down the sides of my face but I stood there and faced the Little Loxwood audience dishevelled in my sailor dress.

I saw my Mummy standing up clapping her face drenched with tears. Aunty Shirley put an arm around her shoulders for a moment and then let go and continued her enthusiastic applause. Granny and Nanna were also standing side by side clapping and smiling at each other. Grandad towered behind Michael clapping and cheering heartily. I could hear him calling out, "Well done Spangle! That's my girl!"

Michael, dwarfed in his huge wheelchair was jamming his fingers into his mouth as he tried to do an appreciative whistle.

In my young life I had never experienced such an overload of attention. Its love and warmth enveloped me and my smile involuntarily stretched right across my face. I bowed once again and then stepped back to the side of the stage as some Scouts came forward and told a few jokes as us younger ones snuck out backwards to get changed into our uniforms ready to do the Grand Finale.

My moment was over so fast, but what a moment and what a feeling. I felt loved. I felt part of something. I felt so proud to be a Brownie Guide. It took no time for us to all put our pressed uniforms on, adjust our sashes and berets and march back onto the stage.

The finale was a medley of bits of all the songs we had sung so far with a new one stuck on the end. It was lighthearted and felt easy now that the rest of the show and my solo were over. Our Scout & Guide Troop flags were held up by the tallest children including Stephen, Dawn's crush. Some at the back had tambourines, shakers or percussion instruments. It was invigorating and we all relaxed into it, holding hands and beaming at each other.

All the Brownies, Cubs, Guides and Scouts were comrades for the few minutes of that wonderful performance. The Grand

Finale was joyous and uplifting. It got noisier as we approached the end of the medley, as we all tapped into the confidence boost we had enjoyed and we proudly showed off in front of our families and neighbours one final time. Needless to say, there was a standing ovation so we had to sing the chorus and the last verse again! The whole performance was physically exhausting.

As the audience were clapping for the second time the Minister came back on stage beaming sweatily. He introduced and thanked Brown Owl, Tawney Owl and the Scout Leaders and all us kids gave them all a hip-hip-hooray!

My Brownie uniform was dripping with sweat and we were all laughing and joking as we collapsed off the stage back into the room behind, jostling and telling each other how great we all were and what fun that had been and did you see this and what about when that happened?

Dawn's make up had splurged itself across her face reminiscent of a crazed clown and she was overly excited and flushed due to the proximity of Stephen the Scout as much as the success of the event.

My cheeks ached from smiling so much and Tammy was also grinning from ear to ear as we threw ourselves down onto the uncomfortable wooden benches. Stacey, Sarah and some of the others from my pack came over and said kind things about my performance.

"Yeah you were amazing Spangle!" Dawn agreed.

"It was like A Night at the London Palladium on the telly." said Stacey. "Only better cos we were in it!!" We were all a bit breathless and giddy.

Some Guides put a jug of orange squash and some beakers on the tables and we gulped it down. Dawn caught sight of her reflection in the mirror and screamed and then laughed and then said crossly, "One of you could have said something."

"About what?" Tammy asked with mock innocence.

"My face. I look like a monster from Scooby Doo." Dawn whined and we all burst out laughing.

"Nothing new there then." Stacey ribbed her and we all thought this was the funniest line ever. Even Dawn cracked a scary looking smile.

CHAPTER THIRTY SIX

There was party food for children and their families in the side room after the performance. I piled up a coloured paper plate with cheesy quavers, cheese and pineapple on sticks and paste sandwiches. Delicious! I filled one for Michael with his favourite things- cocktail sausages, party rings and pink wafers and took it over to him in his wheelchair. My Grandad lit up when he saw me. I felt a mixture of shyness and importance.

"My my!" he said, "What a performance. I had no idea there was so much talent in the family!" then catching his wife's shift in demeanour added. "You obviously take after your grandmother!" and gave a huge cheeky smile. He bent down and gave me a cuddle and then pretended to steal a biscuit from Michaels' plate.

Granny Viv beckoned me to her and then stooped and deposited a kiss on the top of my head.

"Look at your beautiful curls." She purred running her talons through them gently. "You shone like a proper little star out there Spangle. I felt very proud of you. Treading the boards like a trooper"

"Yes we all did. Very proud." added Nanna coming towards me and giving me one of her bristly kisses.

"It was a fabulous show." Mummy said. "Well done Spangle, very well done. You didn't put a foot or a note wrong." She was tearing up again but I felt so happy to have made Mummy proud and she did look very proud. In fact she looked happier than I had seen her all summer and she was also finally eating. She nibbled on a sausage roll and there were some sandwiches on her plate which I was very pleased to see.

At that moment the Minister came over and Nanna introduced Granny to him and the three of them chatted and drifted off

215

towards the tea urn. Some of Michael's friends came and started pushing him around the hall. One climbed on the back of the sturdy old chair and they giggled as it spun around in a slow cumbersome circle.

I could see Aunty Cathy on the other side of the hall talking to a smartly dressed man of about her own age. She was smiling and looking down coyly at her cup and saucer when he spoke to her.

Aunties Doreen, Shirley and Shelia came over to talk to Mummy.

"Well done Spangle." Aunty Doreen said.

"Well we all saw a new side to you today Samantha." said Aunty Shirley knowingly though I had no idea what she actually meant by that. They had brought Mummy a cup of coffee with some Jaffa Cakes perched in the saucer and they all sat down together on the wooden seats in a gossipy cluster.

Grandad sat down nearby and beckoned me to come and sit on his lap which I did. He asked me how long I had been going to Brownies and how long it had taken to learn all the songs and dance steps. Noisy chatter drifted from Mummy and her friends but then hushed as Granny returned with her fresh cup of tea.

Grandad felt her presence so stood up and said, "My, my, well ladies. Will anyone be wanting a lift back down the road?"

"Maybe we should offer Gwen and Cathy a lift home and leave Julie and the children here with their friends for a while. We can come back and pick them up on the way back?"

"Yes Viv, good idea. I'll go and ask Gwen if she would like that." He sauntered off to find Nanna.

"Mummy can I go outside with the others?"

"Of course Spangle but stay in the Chapel grounds. We'll go back home when Grandad and Granny come back. Have you had enough to eat? Maybe take a few more sandwiches?"

"Ok." I said and grabbed a couple more on my way out to the lawned area at the side of the chapel. There were fine roses in full bloom in beds next to the redbrick wall. They clambered along the side of the building along prepositioned wires and pegs. They were bright white with yellow inside and the aroma was delicate but lovely. Someone must have been watering them this very hot summer. My friends were lying on the grass underneath, uniforms un-buttoned and leather belts now removed and deposited in mothers' handbags.

I found a spot among them and lay on my back too. The sun was bright and the sky mainly blue but clouds were puffing across my eyeline, disappearing over the dark pointed roof of the chapel. A breeze ruffled the slightly yellowing leaves on the rose bushes and felt pleasant on my still flushed face. My curls were much looser now and all of us had had our make-up removed so that we looked like little girls again.

No one was saying much. We were tired, I think I could easily have drifted off to sleep on the faint hum of bees buzzing in the flowers and children's laughter.

"I can't believe the summer holidays are nearly over." Tammy said wistfully. "Back to school in two days time."

Where had the weeks disappeared to? So much had happened and it seemed impossible to comprehend that they could ever go back to normal.

"I wonder who our teacher will be?" I said to Dawn.

"I hope it's Miss Goodrich." She said. "She's the kindest in top class."

"Michael will be coming up to Juniors. Ugghh." I said.

"That's funny because he still seems so babyish. Will he be coming in that wheelchair?" Tammy asked.

"He is getting much better on his crutches but I suppose he will need it for getting back and fore. His friends are all arguing over who is going to push him!" I smiled at the thought of a gaggle of little schoolboys pushing the huge black crate down the road to the school crossing. What would the lollipop lady think? Undoubtedly she would be kind and ask him all about what had happened. He would be the centre of attention, just as he is today. He will love it.

"Spangle, it's time to go home." Mummy suddenly called out to me from the entrance gate. I could see my grandparents wagon parked right in front and my grandfather was in front of the open boot folding up Michael's wheelchair and putting it inside. Michael and Granny were already seated within.

"Bye everyone." I said to my little group of Brownie friends as I got up from the grass and walked over to my family.

"Bye bye dancing queen." said Dawn. I laughed and waved. Mummy had my stage dresses in the see through bag and she shooed me into the back seat before getting in beside me.

"We're lucky you have such a large car." Mummy said to her Dad. Granny was lighting up a cigarette and saying, "Hurry Up George. I'm parched. I need a cup of decent tea."

"We're only going a hundred yards down the road Viv." said my Grandad as he got in and shut the door. We pulled out of Larch Road left onto Aspen Way. Grandad was right, it was a very short journey to our house. As he turned into Sycamore Drive there were only a few other cars parked on our street. But my heart froze as I noticed, parked a few yards before the front of our own house, the little dark green car my Daddy drove. No one else seemed to have registered it. Grandad passed round it and parked his bulky estate right in front of it by our gate without giving it a second glance. It was empty.

CHAPTER THIRTY SEVEN

Mummy carefully helped Michael get out of the car whilst Grandad went to the boot to take the wheelchair out. Mummy had his elbow and gently eased him up the steps. He leant on her but made his own way slowly towards the house. I followed them up the path but hung back a little. Granny was stubbing out her cigarette on the garden wall before making her way behind me up the path. Mummy put her key in the lock and pushed the door open then lifted Michael up the step by his underarms. His crutches were inside against the wall next to the door and he reached out for them. Mummy was next to him trying to help him. I could hear my grandmother behind me saying something about tea as I took the step up to enter the hallway.

Then it happened. Quickly, like a tornado, like a purple faced dervish my Dad came flying out of the front room. He pushed my brother to one side and grabbed my mother violently. He pulled her close to him so tightly she could not move as he dragged her back towards the front room door. He half pushed her in and twisted himself around so he was above her. Looking down into her terrified face, his own only inches away from hers.

"Where do you think you've been, you spiteful bitch?" he hissed at her. "Out all day playing happy families with your fancy fat man? Eh? Have you ?" He had hold of her head with one hand and was pulling her hair back with the other. He spat the words into her face. I started crying and so did Michael. Frightened I stepped back out of the hall and nearly fell down the step. My Grandmother caught me and said, "Be careful Spangle for heaven's sake." Then she looked into the house instantly absorbing the scene in front of her. Calmly she strode forwards and said in a loud but composed manner to my Dad "Get your filthy, wretched hands off my daughter. This instant!" His back was half to her and he was completely taken by surprise. He froze for a few seconds. She marched right up to him and tapped him firmly on the shoulder. "Did you hear me Brian?" she said very coldly.

He let my Mummy go and she fell backwards into the door frame. He turned to face my Grandmother squarely.

"Well, if it isn't my favourite in -laws." He smirked as my Grandad appeared at the front door with the wheelchair.

"What's going on here?" my Grandad shouted. He stormed into the hallway past me and Michael. We hardly all fitted into the small space. Fearing the worst I was out on the doorstep ready to run for help if need be.

My Grandad was seeing red. He started to lose his temper. "I said what's going on here? Have you laid a hand on my daughter Brian?" he marched over to Daddy who kept his full height but who clearly looked alarmed and knew that he was not in the best position.

"Answer me!" he growled like a bear.

"Now don't go misinterpreting the situation." my father replied. "Just an exchange of words. Just a few words between a man and his wife George. Just like you and Princess Margaret there. All couples fall out from time to time"

My grandmother made an incongruous sound, stepped forward in front of her own husband and slapped Daddy sharply right across the face. He lost his footing a little and stepped back but soon raised his hand as if to slap her back. My Grandfather moved fast and snatched hold of his raised hand. He looked Daddy square in the face as he twisted it and then pushed him in a single nifty turn ready to eject him straight out of the house.

Michael and I had both stopped crying and Mummy was pulling herself up and trying to stand up straight.

"Tell him Julie. Just a tiff, a few words between man and wife."
Mummy didn't say anything back in return. Her mother walked
past my Dad and put her arms around her daughter and took
her into the front room. Then she called back. "Come on in
children. Come into the front room away from that nasty
excuse for a man." Michael moved along quickly on his
crutches and I followed him in.

"This clearly isn't the first time you have raised your hands and
laid them on a woman." I heard my Grandad say to him. "To
think I thought better of you. Well I was wrong, make sure you
don't darken this door again Brian. I will be instructing my
solicitors first thing tomorrow." Grandads tone was reasonable
but with an aggressive edge to it. He still had my Dad in a
hold.

"Make sure YOU don't darken this door." My Dad replied.
"This is my house and if that bitch thinks she's getting her
hands on it she's got another thing coming."

There was some stumbling and I think my Grandad may have
pushed Dad towards the front door which was still wide open. I
looked at Mummy's startled face. She cast her eyes down to
the hideous swirling carpet at her feet and I thought how
defeated and frail she looked.

"I'm not afraid of solicitors. I've got my own." Daddy said

My grandmother stood up and marched back to the hall door.

"Get out you nasty piece of vermin!" she sneered at him.
"Take your threats elsewhere. Decent people aren't afraid of
the likes of you. If you come here again I shall be calling the
police."

My Dad was laughing. "Call them, call them now if you like!
Nah I've got better things to do. So I'm off now anyway. Call
the police. Ha! But I'll be back. I'm telling you now. I am telling
all of you. I'll be back in my own home"

"I feel sorry for you Brian." My grandmother said. "You not only missed your daughters' wonderful performance this afternoon but now you have also managed to mar her entire day. Well I've got news for you young man. I will not stand by and let you wreck my grandchildren's lives! I will NOT."

She had silenced him. "Clear off!" my grandfather said angrily. But my Dad didn't move from his spot outside the front door.

"Spangle?" he called to me. His voice was softer. I didn't move or reply. "Spangle? Michael? You both forgive Dad the Bad don't you?"

"Clear off Brian!" my Grandad repeated, this time slamming the front door closed.

"Kids?" he tried one more time, through the letterbox of the closed front door, "you still love your old Dad don't you? Spangle?" He called the name he had made up for me in a plaintive strangulated yelp. Then he let the metal letterbox cover drop.

And then it was quiet and then he was gone. For the time being.

CHAPTER THIRTY EIGHT

My grandparents stayed at our house with us that evening. They had decided not to go back to their hotel or to go home just yet. My grandmother made the tea and then she ran a nice bath for my Mum and put her to bed early. Mummy had been crying a lot and she seemed to be overwhelmed with her own Mother's unexpected display of care for her.

My Grandfather went down the road to use the phone box at the parade of shops and when he came back me and Michael were in our nightclothes watching telly. He had bought us each a Milky Way at the pub's off licence when he had stopped in to get some cigarettes.

"I spoke with Cathy." He told my grandmother. "Gwen will come over in the morning and sit with the children whilst we take Julie into town to speak to a solicitor. The sooner we legally get Brian out of her life the better." He plonked himself into my Daddy's chair and lit up two cigarettes, one for him and one for his wife.

"Keep your voice down George, Julie is sleeping and the children, well I expect they have heard enough for one day."

"Of course dear." He said handing her the lit cigarette. "Bridge on the River Kwai is about to start. Now that's what I call a decent film."

"I think I'll take the children up to bed now. Give your Grandad a kiss goodnight." Granny said as she helped Michael to his feet. I was tired and glad to get to bed. Granny tucked Michael in first after overseeing our teeth cleaning and then she came and sat down on my bed. She asked me if I had said my prayers and I told her I had. I had only done the short version and I would do a proper one when she was gone downstairs.

She took my hand and told me that she thought I had been marvellous in the show and that I had 'shone like a star'. We both looked out of the window and we could see a few early evening stars twinkling there already.

"You must try not to worry about grown-up affairs Spangle." She told me. "Grown ups make lots of silly mistakes but children shouldn't have to worry about those. Children should think about children's things like what is a rainbow made of and things like that. Everything will turn out well. You must trust me on this." She gave me a kiss.

I didn't say anything but snuggled deep into my pillow. The hall light cast a shape of yellow gold across her as she stood up. "Night, night, sweet dreams" she said, just like Mummy always did.

As she left the room I heard Michael calling her. He was having a nosebleed and she calmly went to the bathroom to dampen a flannel for him. I got up and closed my door and leant my chin on the windowsill and looked out for a few minutes. The houses at the back had their lights on but one of them had all their curtains closed tight. In the other I could see a cat curled up on a cushion in front of a flickering television. There was a lady on a comfy looking armchair flicking through a magazine. She was wearing a bright pink quilted nylon housecoat with matching slippers and she had curlers in her hair. The man was in the kitchen window at the sink. He was wearing a white round necked vest. It looked like he was doing the washing up.

I got back into bed and started on the full extended version of that night's prayer. It took ages because there was a lot to thank God for, but I needed to ask him quite a few times if he could hurry up with making everything turn out right. I didn't want to complain but this really was taking a long, long time and I didn't know how much more Mummy could take. I thanked him for the gang show and for helping Michael learn to walk so well so soon. I thanked him for the Milky Way and for my health and for my family. I thanked him for my friends and I asked him to look after Herbert in heaven. Then for the

225

final time I asked him please to make everything turn out right Amen. Then I turned over and listened to the sounds of the house as my breathing slowed and I floated off to sleep.

CHAPTER THIRTY NINE

The house felt over full with people the next morning as Nanna arrived first thing and Mummy got fused over and bullied into getting ready to go with her parents to meet a solicitor.

"For goodness sake Julie, you must have something smarter to wear than that" my grandmother said horrified at her summer dress and cardigan ensemble. "We can't take you to meet a solicitor looking like a battered wife!"

"She is a battered wife." My Grandad said helpfully.

"George!" she admonished him with her expression and tone of voice as she applied her face powder and finished off with her signature lipstick.

Nanna was very quiet and solemn with me and Michael after they all finally left amid a flurry of bickering.

Michael was now flying around the house on his crutches, swinging his legs and moving like a dervish. He seemed to love this unique thing about himself and he raced around the place like an over animated cartoon character, hopping over coffee tables and pouffes as if he were completing an obstacle course. He was driving Nanna mad so she let him go out and call for Robert.

I didn't want to say in the house either and although much cooler and cloudier today I also decided to put on a cardigan and go and see which gang members were about on our last day but one of summer freedom. Dawn wasn't at home, her brother said she had gone shopping in town with her Mummy. So I went round the block and knocked on Tammy's door. Sarah was there already and we all three put a blanket on her lawn and sat outside playing with her Sindy's in the watery morning sunshine. There was quite a bit of shade from their trellis fencing and I felt chilly in the garden. There was a feeling of a summer coming to an end and the smell of Autumn on the breeze. We were all looking forward to going back to school now that the show was over but we were also apprehensive about what our new teachers would be like and being back in our routines.

The collection of Sindys were set out in a row as we pretended to do a Miss World competition with them. Tammy had five and Sarah had also bought two along. As they all had the exact same complexions, faces and bodies it was really only their hair and costumes that we could judge them on. We spent some time preparing them all to look their best, but different from each other, changing their little plastic shoes and making tiny adjustments to their hair. Tammy had a wide range of clothes for us to pick from in garish colours and to suit every season.

We each pretended to be one of them at a time as we went through a line up. Then we gave them a few superficial personality traits and world views as we interviewed each others chosen dolls. Choosing their country of origin was fun. I wasn't bothered about being Miss UK though both of the others wanted to be her. Although I loved the summer and warmth I was attracted to the idea of being Miss Antarctica or Miss Finland or somebody from other cold places that I knew nothing about. The UK was far too boring a choice for me.

Heads down in a world of our own we played happily at this game for ages, racially stereotyping to our hearts content as we tried to make sense of the complexities of women's place and value in our own smaller world. We all implicitly understood the importance of being looked at, of playing the game of femininity and beauty.

Miss UK won in the end as the other two out voted me but I didn't really mind. My tummy was rumbling and it was time to head home for some lunch.

They weren't back from town yet and Nanna had made me and Michael sausage sandwiches with ketchup which were quite delicious. We also had Angel Delight for pudding which was quite a treat- butterscotch flavour with a few slices of banana hidden beneath. I helped Nanna with the washing up as Michael went back out to play. She looked sad so I asked her if she would like a cup of tea and set about making a pot.

Nanna sat at the wiped down Formica kitchen table as I placed her favourite cup and saucer in front of her. I had my Bay City Rollers mug and I filled both with strong reddish tea. She put a drop of milk in each and a spoonful of sugar in hers as she had a sweet tooth. She had her magazine unopened in front of her, 'The People's Friend' it had a nice painting on the cover of a cottage and watermill by a flowing stream. I went and fetched my Jackie comic from the front room but neither of us felt like reading.

"Would you like to help me do the puzzle?" Nanna asked.

"It might be too hard for me. I could read you something?" I suggested.

"Yes please, my eyes are tired. I'd like you to read me the story if you don't mind. The one near the beginning with the picture of the cat."

I gladly read her the story of a lady who lived alone in a village post office. The lady lost her little tabby cat but was reunited with it when a handsome postman discovered him in his sack.

She smiled at the ending and refilled her cup. Nanna must get very lonely sometimes, I thought. I felt suddenly sorry for her and went across and gave her a cuddle.

Then the front door opened and Mummy and my grandparents noisily returned. I refilled the kettle and swilled out the pot as they came into the kitchen to tell Nanna all about their morning in town. My Grandmother's perfume arrived a few seconds before they all did. Then she pulled out and flounced down dramatically into a kitchen chair.

"Well Gwen, I am sorry to have to tell you that divorce papers will be served on Brian by hand today at Hartley's department store, his place of work." Grandma said in a way that sounded anything but sorry.

"This very afternoon. In fact, it could even be now." She glanced down at her delicate bracelet wristwatch.

"I see." Nanna replied quietly. Mummy went to her and squeezed her hand.

"I'm sorry Gwen, he gave me no other choice."

"You do not need to say sorry. You are not accountable to me Julie, only to God." Nanna said sadly. The room was quiet until the kettle began to whistle hysterically.

"Thank you Spangle" Granny said to me as I placed the fresh pot down on the table. My grandad sat down and patted at his lap to signal me to go over to him and sit down with him. Mummy got out more cups and saucers.

"Hopefully Brian will see sense and will not contest it. He is the wrong doer and this could all be over reasonably quickly if he accepts that." Mummy sighed after her mother had given this little speech to the table.

"Then we can all get on with our lives!" Granny concluded with a flourish.

"I don't imagine he will be happy to be served legal papers at work." Mummy said.

"Well if we don't know where he is living Julie, I don't see that he left us any choice. If it is embarrassing for him for this to happen at his place of work, then so be it. This entire situation is embarrassing for all of us."

"It's heart breaking, not embarrassing." said Gwen standing up and pushing her cup and saucer forward.

"I think it's time I was on my way Julie." She said looking directly at Mummy.

"I, I'll walk you to the bus stop Gwen." Mummy said.

"Very well. Yes, I would appreciate that."

"This changes nothing between us Gwen. You will always be family. You are the children's Nanna." My mother tried to placate her.

"I can't talk about it Julie, not at present. Let me get my things. I feel too ….." she sobbed as Mummy left the room with her. Granny Viv lit up a cigarette for herself and one for my Grandad and they both sat there puffing and sipping their tea. I got up and opened the window. I breathed in a gulp of fresh air. I felt the comfort of it's coolness on my face.

"It's not my fault if she's an over sensitive woman George, so don't look at me like that." My grandmother said to her husband.

"I said nothing my dear." He replied sweetly.

"Not one word."

CHAPTER FORTY

My grandparents decided that their business here was concluded for today and that they would go back to their hotel to get a good night's sleep. They said that they would come back round in the morning to see us and say goodbye properly before going back to where they lived on the other side of the country.

Mummy was silent and crest fallen on her return from taking Nanna to the bus stop. She looked relieved to see them go. She set up the ironing board and started sorting out our clothes and PE kits and other things ready for school. I read my book in the front room and watched her as thoughts chased through her mind and then across her face.

Aunty Shirley popped in and gave my Mum a jar of coffee as a present.

"Pop the kettle on Samantha love" she instructed and I went to the kitchen and did as I was told as Mummy bought her up to speed on the days proceedings.

"D.I.V.O.R.C.E. gosh. I never thought it would really happen." Aunty Shirley said spelling it out in the delusion that I didn't know exactly what they were talking about.

"How are you feeling Julie love?"

"I don't know. Numb I suppose."

"Hmmm"

"I just wish it was all over and done with. It still seems unreal and uncertain. Gwen is terribly upset Shirley."

"It's not about Gwen, or other people, it's about you and your kids."

"And Brian" Mummy said flatly.

Aunty Shirley didn't stay long and at least Mummy knew that she wouldn't have to go through the ordeal of telling the other neighbours as Shirley was probably already in the process of doing just that.

Mummy looked out of the window vacantly. It was starting to get a little dark.

"Can you go and find Michael and tell him it's time to come in Spangle and I will make your tea."

Off I went to do as I was told. Michael was on the green with Robert and some others. They were laughing carelessly and he was swinging from his crutches and playing the joker. He made a weak protest about it still being early but then followed me home anyway. Mummy had made us beans on toast which we ate at the table and then she helped Michael up the stairs so we could go and get ready for bed before watching some telly. The living room felt colder than it had done and we put our little dressing gowns and slippers on before snuggling up on the sofa. Mummy put the gas fire on for five minutes to 'take the chill off'. Mummy had pushed the pouffe up close to the sofa so that Michael could have his leg up and be comfortable. There was nothing much on so Mummy switched the box off and we all had a game of Chinese chequers. I loved that game, Nanna had taught me lots of 'tactics' so I always had a good chance of winning which would make Michael so cross and angry that it was almost funny. We had three games and all won one each and then it was bedtime.

But as I was putting the counters back in the holes and tidying the game away my neck hairs tingled as I picked up the familiar and frightening sound of a key in the lock. My stomach started churning as we all fell silent and looked towards the living room door.

Mummy pushed me behind her and stood up in front of us, head held high as Daddy walked through the door in his familiar suede jacket. He had a suitcase in his hand which he carefully placed down on the floor.

"Hello kids!" he smiled showing us the gap between his two front teeth. "Aren't you going to say hello to Dad the Bad?" Michael poked his head forward and half smiled but then pulled back behind Mummy.

"All ready for bed I see." he said nicely.

"I was just about to take them up Brian." Mummy said in a reasonable tone. "We weren't expecting you."

"Well here I am. Under the instructions of my solicitor. I am moving back into my house Julie. I am asserting my right to live here. "

"I think you gave up that right by your actions."

"I am not going to rise to any bait. I am just going to go up and unpack then I can put the kids to bed for you. Bedtime story Michael?"

Michael smiled broadly and then nodded. Mummy didn't move for a moment and then she stepped aside and looked at us and said.

"Alright kids, up you go. I will come and tuck you in after Daddy has read you a story." She must had read on my face that I didn't feel as delighted as Michael did at this prospect so she leant down and kissed me saying. "It's OK Spangle, I'll be up in a minute."

Daddy helped Michael up giving him lots of kind praise about how well he was moving about. "What a solider you are son! Just like your old Dad." he beamed at Michael's happy face.

I heard Mummy quietly slip out the back door. She was only gone a few moments and if Daddy noticed he didn't let on. I was listening to every sound and calculated she had dashed two doors down to Aunty Shirley's. She was back within a few short minutes and came straight upstairs and stood at the door of Michaels room watching as Daddy read us a story about the ducklings of New York. Daddy was calm and kind. He ruffled Michaels hair and asked him if he was comfortable. He made some jokes about hop-a-long Cassidy. I sat on the edge of the bed behind him and I turned and gave Mummy a half smile.

When Daddy, sensing her there, turned around suddenly I nearly jumped out of my skin. But he did nothing. He did not move. He smiled at me and sat there calmly.

"Right Spangle, it's your bedtime now." he said. "Let's give Michael some peace and quiet."

"One more story?" Michael pushed it but Daddy placidly said,

"Not tonight son. Get some sleep."

"Night, Night." Michael murmured as Mummy gave him a kiss before we left the room and Mummy gently closed his door.

They both came into my room and said good night and gave me kisses and then I heard Mummy and Daddy going into their bedroom next door to mine.

"You've nothing to worry about Julie. Don't stand there like a rabbit in the headlights. My solicitor has told me not to lay a hand on you. I am following his instructions like the good boy that I am." You could clearly hear the self-mockery in his tone of voice.

"I see" Mummy said quietly. There was a knock on the front door and Mummy went down to answer it. I could hear my Grandfathers voice in the hallway below asking Mummy what was going on.

"Ask him yourself, Dad. He says he's moving back in under the instructions of his solicitors."

My Dad emerged from their bedroom and went down the stairs towards them.

"That's right father-in-law. I've got a solicitor too you know. Thanks for the hand delivered letter by the way. Nice to know you're all thinking about me."

"You shameless, sarcastic ……..You're not worth it Brian. I'm glad you've got a solicitor. The sooner we get this divorce finalised the better."

"What if I don't want a divorce?" Daddy mocked in his sweetest voice. "What if I am perfectly happy with things the way they are?"

"It's not your happiness I am concerned about I am afraid Brian." They moved into the front room and I could hear less of what they were saying. But although I felt less frightened now that I knew my grandfather was here, I still couldn't get to sleep.

I heard Grandad's voice raised once or twice but not for long. After a while I heard my Dad come upstairs. He used the toilet and the bathroom and then went into the bedroom. He moved around, probably putting his pyjamas on and then it was quiet in there. I dozed a little but was keeping vigilant. Mummy and Grandad were still talking downstairs. I heard them go into the kitchen and the sound of the kettle going on the stove and then I fell asleep again. I think I woke a little later in the night and heard them still talking before oblivion finally came for me.

CHAPTER FORTY ONE

When I woke up again my Mummy was in bed with me. It was staring to get light outside and I could see her chestnut hair spread lusciously on my purple synthetic pillowcase. The house was quiet, but birds were singing outside my window. I could smell my mother's fragrance and she was warm next to me. I didn't want to wake her so I closed my eyes and listened. A car drove past outside its engine sounds fading away down the street. I detected what might have been a dog walker as a faint tinkle of what could have been a dog tag against a collar floated by.

Then I heard Daddy moving around in his bedroom, opening the curtains and then a window. He coughed a smoker's cough and went noisily to the toilet. Then he clumped downstairs. Mummy stirred. Her eyes were puffy and she looked like she had been crying but she gave me a warm smile, like the morning sun.

"Gosh, what time is it?" she said reaching to the bedside table for her watch. "I can't laze around all day, it's past eight o'clock." She said mostly to herself.

"Is Grandad still here?" I asked her.

"No but he'll be here soon with Granny."

She registered sounds from downstairs signifying Daddy was up.

"Daddy hasn't gone to work today then." she said, again almost as if she was talking to herself. I opened the curtains. It looked cloudy and grey. The tree at the back corner of the garden was swaying in a strong breeze. Mummy looked out and said "O dear, looks like a jumper day today already."

She went to help Michael as I got washed and dressed but I waited upstairs until she was ready to go down as I didn't want to be with my Daddy on my own. But when we came down he simply said, "Morning all!" and went upstairs to wash and dress himself.

We ate a quiet breakfast, Michael making quite a mess with his Rice Krispies as he greedily ate like a starving orphan. I nibbled on my toast unable to look at him as he had a milk moustache and milk made me queasy. I was worried about Daddy coming back downstairs and shouting at us or getting cross and could not understand why he hadn't gone to work as usual.

Before we finished eating though my grandparent's car rolled grandly and serenely up outside the house and Mummy rushed to the front door to let them in.

I heard my Grandad asking her if anything had happened and she said no as they both bustled through to the kitchen to say good morning to us.

"Michael, you have breakfast cereal in your hair! Really, whatever next?" Were my Grandmother's first words as my mother followed her in and put the kettle on.

"Where's that wretched man Julie?" she said before anyone had replied to her first question.

"Upstairs"

"Well this is most unsatisfactory. Isn't it? Most unsatisfactory. George. Off you go now. Julie your father just needs to go and make a few phone calls. Talk to the solicitor on the telephone if he will answer on a Bank Holiday Monday and I will stay here with you and the children."

"Of course Mum. Here's your tea."

"It's stewed Julie. I can't drink that. Please make a fresh pot. Good job you had a cup at the hotel George. What are you still hanging about here for like a lost soul? Off you go George."

"Yes dear." He said kissing her coiffured hair.

"I didn't get a wink of sleep last night." She continued. "This really is all too frightful. What you ever saw in that man is beyond me. And you look like you've been dragged through a hedge backwards too Julie. Putting us through all this. Really. Just all too much."

Mummy put another cup of tea before her as she lit up a cigarette.

"I spoke to your brother Nigel on the phone last night Julie and he just can't believe any of this. And your Uncle Ernest and Aunty Edna are devastated. Devastated. Just devastated. I do hope George isn't going to take too long."

"You phoned Nigel in Australia?" Mummy was clearly shocked.

"I know, the expense was ridiculous. Where is that dreadful man? I take it he's in this house?"

"Upstairs, he's upstairs. I wish you wouldn't tell everyone Mum. Things aren't even finalised yet."

"Upstairs! Barefaced cheek!"

"Who else have you told?"

"No one Julie. Shame faced cheek, here in this house!"

"Thought my ears were burning. Welcome to MY house mother-in-law." Daddy entered the kitchen with a cocky grin.

"Coffee for me Julie. Gone off tea since I've travelled to Europe. They all drink coffee on the continent don't you know?"

My Grandmother almost spat out her tea.

"Make your own coffee!" she snarled. "Come on everyone, in the other room I can't be cooped up in here in such bad company."

239

"Bloody snob, now I know where *she* gets it from." Daddy said tilting his head towards my mother. He just couldn't stop himself from retaliating.

My grandmother looked him up and down coldly. But she said nothing and turned her back on him as she marched into the living room.

"Morning Spangle! Bet you're glad to have Dad the Bad home aren't you?"

I gave him a non-committal half smile and scurried into the front room. Mummy helped Michael upstairs to give him another wash and clean up and Daddy busied himself loudly in the kitchen making himself a big breakfast of scrambled eggs and sausages.

My grandmother was silently furious and she gave all her attention to me as she helped me do some colouring in my Woolworths colouring book, adding decorative flourishes around the edges of the page and outside of the lines of the picture.

My Dad flicked on the radio and was whistling along to the pop songs as he nosily banged pots and pans to goad her. After a while though we did both ignore him and Mummy and Michael eventually both came back down.

"What's taking George so long?" my grandmother asked no one in particular. Then she called out to my Dad, "No work today Brian? How are you going to afford my daughter's maintenance if you can't be bothered to work?"

"Mum! Ssshh " my mother said. Daddy had turned the radio off and was stood in the doorway. He looked as if he were about to explode. He filled the frame with an arm on each side. He looked totally menacing but Granny held his stare. He broke eye contact first and looked around the room at his family.

He glared at us all. I wanted to vomit with fear, Michael was ashen. Still Daddy stood there, tensed, saying nothing, with pure hatred oozing from his every pore.

"It's a Bank Holiday. A day of rest, for your information Princess Margret, Mrs High and Bloody Mighty. O and by the way if that bitch thinks she's getting one single penny out of me, she's mistaken." he snarled. The house quivered slightly as he turned his back on us and violently slammed the kitchen door.

"Charming. I'm sure." My grandmother shouted at the closed door.

"Please, stop provoking him." Mummy said in her quietest voice.

"Shut up Julie, I'll say what I want to whomever I want. I am no doormat!" she turned back to me though and we carried on colouring in a woodland scene to which she had now added a few extra birds nest building in a tree.

Finally, I saw my grandad's car through the front window and breathed a quiet sigh of relief. Mummy went to let him in. He looked very sombre as he came into the living room. He sat down on the pouffe in the middle of us all and looked at his wife.

"I finally managed to get old Mr Hodgekinson on the phone. His wife gave me the number of his golf club. It's not good news I'm afraid Viv." he said to his wife's impatient face. "Brian is the legal tenant of this property and can only be asked to leave if he breaches the tenancy or breaks the law."

"No!" my grandmother gasped.

"Julie can only take on the tenancy if he willingly signs it over to her, or if Brian becomes incapacitated in some way and even then, it is at the discretion of the local corporation"

There was a grim laugh from behind the closed kitchen door.

241

Mummy's eyes reddened and filled with tears but she didn't quite cry.

"If Julie wants to remain in this house then......." Daddy opened the kitchen door "........then she's only too welcome. Of course she can stay. She can remain here with me as my wife."

"Good God no!" my grandmother gasped. "Where's your sense of decency man?" he laughed right back at her.

"I have none. I am a good for nothing wretch, remember?"

"Would you turn out your own children?"

"No. Haven't I said they can all stay here with me? You'd like that wouldn't you kids? That's what we all want isn't it? Happy families."

No one said anything.

"Just been through a bit of a rocky patch that's all."

"And what about your mistress? Rita? What does she think of all this?" Granny asked vitriolically.

"Rita understands."

"Understands what?" my Grandad asked this time standing up to his full height and looking at my father like he was some incomprehensible organism from an alien planet.

"She knew I was married from the start, she knows the score. Rita is a woman of the world."

"What are you saying man? That you would live here with my daughter and grandchildren and continue to carry on seeing this woman?"

Mummy got up and left the room, she rushed up the stairs and I could hear her being sick in the toilet. I wanted to go to her but I was too scared to move.

"I can't listen to this imbecile a moment longer. He has no basic human decency. Brian, I pity you." She said, this time with no spite or harshness and she followed her daughter out of the room and went upstairs.

"That's my final offer George." Daddy said before going back into the kitchen switching the radio back on and finishing his breakfast. Granny appeared in the doorframe of the hall.

"George, look after Michael, Spangle come upstairs with me and help Mummy and I pack."

"Viv?" Grandad asked

"I am not leaving them here with that monster. You heard what he said. They are going to have to come and live with us."

"Yes dear, of course."

"Come Spangle. The spare room will do for the children and we can do something with the box room for Julie. It needed a good sort out anyway. I've made up my mind."

"Quite right, yes dear." He said to his wife as she herded me upstairs. Mummy came out of the bathroom after washing her face. She tied her hair back and gave her mother a questioning look.

"You're all three of you coming with us Julie. I won't take any arguing. Have you any suitcases?"

"There's some under my bed." Mummy said "and some overnight bags under Michaels."

"Well those should do very well. Let's put them on Michaels bed and pack what you need. Your father can come back up another time and get anything we can't get in the car today." She spoke kindly but firmly and we both did as we were told. I had a case to put in toys and games for me and Michael, just a selection of things we play with most and our favourite special things like Michael's teddy and my glass animals.

Granny helped me wrap them up in socks and then place them carefully inside a pillowcase.

We worked quickly and Granny went downstairs to get my Grandad to come up and take them out to the car in order of size, biggest first. The sky outside was black and menacing by now and the wind had whipped up since earlier. I took some carrier bags of shoes and slippers out to him that Mummy had handed me and as I turned to go back into the house, I saw Aunty Shirley poke her head out of her sitting room window.

"Samantha, dear, come here" she called across to me. I wasn't sure what to do. I looked at Grandad and he smiled and nodded so I went over to their house and up the garden path to her.

"What's going on, what are all those suitcases?" she asked

"We are going to go and live with Granny and Grandad." I replied

"What now?"

"Yes, when we have packed the car."

"No! I must come and say goodbye to your mother. How is she? Are you really leaving?" she didn't wait for an answer just pulled her headscarfed covered head back indoors and was soon out of her front door and in front of me heading to my house. She was almost running. I could not keep up with her. As we got to the door my Grandad came out with Michael's crutches and our wellies. Aunty Shirley ignored him and went straight into the house calling my mothers' name.

Mummy was coming down the stairs with a sponge bag in her hands and she stopped when she saw Aunty Shirley.

"You can't just go Julie." She said. "You can't just let him win."

"I've no choice Shirley, really. He won't give up this house. He won't leave so I have to. Me and the children aren't safe living here with him."

"He has to leave. He's in the wrong. It's the only decent thing he can do." She stifled a sob, she was clearly very upset and it was making Mummy upset too. Granny came down the stairs behind Mummy and put an arm on her shoulder.

"He won't go and he doesn't want a divorce. He may contest it."

"Bastard!"

"Quite" my Grandmother agreed and then continued down the stairs past them both. Grandad came back in and then went into the front room to get Michael. He picked him up and gently began to carry him out to the car.

"The weather is turning stormy Julie." Grandad said. "Have you got a blanket that we can wrap the children up in? The heating in this car takes a while to warm up"

"I'll get one Daddy." she said and turned back upstairs.

Aunty Shirley lost control and started shouting.

"Brian, Brian where are you hiding, you nasty bastard? Where are you?" she marched down into the living room and my Grandmother immediately pushed me away further down the hall. Mummy came down with a blanket and she held my hand.

"I want to give you a piece of my mind. How many people have to suffer because of your selfishness?"

I heard the kitchen door open. Granny turned to Mummy and said

"You and Spangle go and get into the car now. I think that's everything packed. Go on Julie. I'll be there in a moment."

"What's going on?" Daddy's voice got louder.

"What do you think is going on you filthy bastard?" I heard Aunty Shirley shout before Mummy got me to my Grandad and he helped me into the car. Michaels face was confused.

"Get in the back on the other side Julie." Grandad said. We all looked towards the storm brewing in the house as the sky darkened outside and the first spots of rain in months began to splash onto the car windows. Granny was at the front door fastening a headscarf around her hair trying to usher Aunty Shirley out of the house but she was making hard work of it as she continued to hurl abuse at my father.

She finally came out onto the path, spat something at my Dad and then rushed down to the car to give Mummy a hug goodbye.

Daddy stumbled out of the house behind her.

"I said what's going on?" he shouted. The sky was cobalt. The wind was building up as a flurry of leaves whipped his sheepskin slippers.

"What's going on here Julie?" Daddy said more quietly, slowly making his way to the top of the steps by the gate. He looked down at us all perplexed as a sudden gust of wind ruffled his mousey hair.

"Get in the car Julie." Grandad said and she did. Sliding in next to Michael whose leg was sticking forward between the two front seats.

"Shirley, could you kindly make sure the wheelchair is returned to the Minister?" he said.

"Of course." Aunty Shirley replied between sobs before shouting "Bastard" at the confused figure of my Dad and then walking off back towards her own house.

"What's happening George, where are you taking all that stuff?"

"We are taking your family Brian, not stuff"

"That's right." Granny said as she opened the door to the front passenger seat. "It's starting to rain Brian you better get in before you catch your death."

"I don't understand." Daddy said quietly, stupidly, almost like a child. Mummy wound down her car window.

"We are leaving you Brian." she said and then wound it back up and looked away.

He looked injured. His body crumpled forwards, he howled, then started to cry. Big, angry tearful cries. Granny got into the car and closed her door.

"It's raining Brian. You need to get indoors." Grandad said not unkindly.

The raindrops were falling faster now but my father stood there in his trousers and vest with only his smelly slippers on his feet crying like a baby. His face was red and blotched and scrunched up like a child having a tantrum.

"Get in George." Grandma instructed her husband. "We need to make a start. We've a long journey ahead."

Daddy came down the steps onto the pavement. "Julie is this what you want? Ten years of marriage down the drain." His perplexed and contorted face was close to the window of the car as he tried to lean towards where my mother was sitting but she kept her face forward. My grandfather started up the engine and Daddy took a step back away from the kerb, his face wet with rain and tears.

The heavens properly opened and distant thunder rumbled but still he stood there crying like his heart was broken and we had all wronged him to the core. Another roar of thunder, closer now and I felt Michael's little body vibrate as he too started to cry quietly. Mummy put her arm around him and kept looking forward towards the trees lashing wildly on the green at the corner of our street. Grandad had started the car and pulled away very slowly. He flicked on the windscreen wipers and slid the lever to crank up the car heater. We juddered down the road in what felt like slow motion. I turned and looked back at the ruined figure of my father. He had gone back up the garden steps and was staring down the road after us weeping and holding his head in his hands as we drove out of Sycamore Drive on the day the rains finally came and the heatwave of 1976 ended.

suzannedavies1313@gmail.com

Printed in Great Britain
by Amazon